I0643124

A. E. C.

Hymns and their Stories

A. E. C.

Hymns and their Stories

ISBN/EAN: 9783744780896

Printed in Europe, USA, Canada, Australia, Japan

Cover: Foto ©Andreas Hilbeck / pixelio.de

More available books at **www.hansebooks.com**

HYMNS

AND THEIR STORIES.

BY

A. E. C.

WITH A PREFACE ·

BY

EDGAR C. S. GIBSON, M.A.,

PRINCIPAL OF THE THEOLOGICAL COLLEGE, WELLS, AND PREBENDARY OF
WELLS CATHEDRAL.

PUBLISHED UNDER THE DIRECTION OF THE TRACT COMMITTEE.

SOCIETY FOR PROMOTING CHRISTIAN KNOWLEDGE,
LONDON : NORTHUMBERLAND AVENUE, W.C. ;
43, QUEEN VICTORIA STREET, E.C.
BRIGHTON: 129, NORTH STREET.
NEW YORK: E. & J. B. YOUNG & CO.
1896.

AUTHOR'S PREFACE.

A CONSIDERABLE portion of this little book was written before Dr. Julian's wonderful and exhaustive work, *The Dictionary of Hymnology*, appeared.

The Author most gratefully acknowledges the great help that the latter book has been in verifying facts, correcting errors, and supplying additional information ; and strongly recommends it for study to all who wish to learn more upon the subject of Hymns.

The Author feels also deeply indebted to Mr. John Murray, who has generously agreed to withdraw his just claim for transgression of his copyright.

PREFACE.

WE are told in Dr. Julian's *Dictionary of Hymn-ology* that "the total number of Christian hymns in the two hundred or more languages and dialects in which they have been written or translated is not less than four hundred thousand "—a fact which bears striking testimony to the position that the singing of hymns holds in the devotions of the Christian Church. And although hymns must always stand or fall by their own merits, and the origin and authorship of many of the noblest of them is unknown, yet there can be no doubt that the interest attaching to a hymn is greatly increased when we are able to refer them to their right authors, and assign them to particular occasions in their lives. We all know what a gain it is to the Psalms when we are permitted to associate them with definite incidents in the life of David, or to illustrate them from the events of the history of Israel. So is it with the hymns which we use in our churches. In many cases there are traditions of no slight interest and beauty—in some cases authentic information is not wanting—in regard to the occasions on which they were composed ; while even to know the names of their authors, and the times at which they lived is sometimes sufficient to suggest associations which give fresh interest to familiar words. To give but a single example. Such hymns as " Brief life is here our portion," and " Jerusalem, the golden," receive a new significance when we recollect that they belong to the age of the Crusades, when " men's hearts were fired with love and devotion to that Master in Whose honour they bore the Red Cross, and Whose tomb they went to rescue from heathen spoilers." With this thought in our minds, we can see at once that "the hymns themselves speak of the time in which they were written—of the glories of the *New* Jerusalem, of peace after war, of rest after battle."[1]

It is no wonder then that the study of Hymnology has proved a fascinating one, and that the works which deal with it are very numerous. Never perhaps was greater interest taken in it than at the present day. In this country the works of Lord Selborne, the late Archbishop Trench, and John Mason Neale did perhaps more than

[1] See p. 60.

anything else to awaken this interest, and promote
a knowledge of the subject, while quite recently a
fresh impetus has been given to the study by the
publication of Dr. Julian's great work already
alluded to, the *Dictionary of Hymnology*, a work in
which full information may be found on an enormous
number of hymns, and on all subjects connected
with them and their authors. This volume, however, is of course designed for the student rather
than for the general reader, and is on too large a
scale to be widely circulated. There was room,
therefore, for a small work which should popularize
the subject, and tell in simple language the story
of the growth of Christian hymnody, assigning,
as far as possible, to their proper dates and authors
those universal favourites which find a place in all
the hymn-books in common use. This work has
been admirably done by A. E. C., who, in this
series of papers, to which I have been asked to
contribute a few words by way of Preface, has
given a very careful sketch of the whole subject—
stopping short designedly before the present day,
so as to exclude reference to living writers in this
country. Portions of some of these papers have
already appeared in the *Dawn of Day*, but they
have been considerably altered and added to, and
are well worth preserving in a permanent form.
They furnish an excellent introduction to a subject

which seems to grow in interest the more it is studied, and the stories collected in them will often be found to furnish new and delightful illustrations of the old truth that—

> "A verse may find him whom a sermon flies,
> And turn delight into a sacrifice."

EDGAR C. S. GIBSON.

Wells, Somerset,
    July 7, 1894.

CONTENTS.

HYMNS

AND THEIR STORIES.

I.

BIBLE HYMNS.

"And when they had sung an hymn."—S. MATT. xxvi. 30. "And at midnight Paul and Silas were praying and sing- ing hymns unto God, and the prisoners were listening to them."—ACTS xvi. 25, R.V. "Speaking to yourselves in psalms and hymns, and spiritual songs ; singing and making melody in your hearts to the Lord."—EPH. v. 19 ; COL. iii. 16.

PERHAPS there is hardly anything which will give us more interest in Church history or make us feel what a grand heritage our Catholic Church possesses, than the study of her hymns. We have to go back into far-off countries, and centuries long ago, and when we find that we are singing the very same grand old hymns which were sung by Apostles, by S. Ambrose, by King Alfred, by S. Patrick, and the saintly Bede, we realize more and more the great doctrine of the Communion of Saints. We have now to speak of Christian hymns ; but we must remember that the old Hebrew songs were the foundation of our hymns, and that the Book of Psalms was the Hymn Book of our Lord and His

Apostles, and the *Great Hallel* probably the last hymn He sang.

The earliest New Testament hymns were the songs of Zacharias and of the Blessed Virgin, the song of the angels at the birth of Christ, and the song of Simeon.

From very early times the Benedictus—" Blessed be the Lord God of Israel "—was used as an early morning hymn. We use it most appropriately after the second lesson in the morning service, when we have just heard the glad news of the Gospel. Still more is the Nunc Dimittis—the song of Simeon—an evening hymn, and from the earliest Christian times it has been sung at vespers. Both these Canticles speak of Christ as *The Light*. In the first, the rising sun—" the dayspring from on high," giving " light to them that sit in darkness and the shadow of death "—is used as a type of Christ ; and the Benedictus may be called the *sunrise* hymn. Bishop Alexander tells us that the figure in the last verse is that of a caravan, which has lost its way in the dark. The travellers wait in the gloom till the sun arises to show them their way. So is the Nunc Dimittis the *sunset* hymn— sleep has always been the type of death—and here Christ is the " Light to lighten the Gentiles," the Light to lighten the dark valley of the shadow of death. The hymn has often been used, too, as a prayer for a holy death, and also as a Post Communion hymn, when our Blessed Saviour has taken up His abode in our hearts.

There used to be a very pretty custom on Candlemas Day, that is, the Feast of the Purification, the day on which the Nunc Dimittis was first sung by

Simeon. The people all took tapers to church, which were lighted at a fire kindled by the Bishop. A rubric of the time of Henry VIII. says :—"On Candlemasse Days it shall be declared that the bearing of candles is done in memorie of Christe, the spiritualle lighte,of whom Simeon did prophecye, as it is read in the Church at this day." There is an old Latin hymn, by Adam of S. Victor, of whom we shall hear later, for the blessing of the candles—

> "As one, love to Jesus bearing,
> In this festal custom sharing,
>   Doth a waxen taper hold ;
> So the Father's Word supernal,
> Pledge of purity maternal,
>   Did old Simeon's arms enfold."

It is a curious fact that, with the great exception of the Magnificat, we hear of scarcely any other Christian hymns written by women until quite modern times. If they were written, the names of their authors remain hidden from us. The resemblance between this song of the Blessed Virgin and the song of Hannah, in the Old Testament, has often been noticed.

The first Christian hymn, in the sense of being the first sung after the Birth of Christ, was the Gloria in Excelsis—the Angels' song, " Glory to God in the highest," etc. Pliny, a writer who lived in the first century after Christ, says that the Christians used "to meet at an early hour, before dawn, to sing a hymn of praise to Christ as God." Many think that this was the Gloria in Excelsis ; and it has even been suggested that it may have been part of the Te Deum, the first ten verses of which have been found in Greek.

S. Chrysostom says : " They met together daily, to
sing their morning hymn, with one mouth, to God ;
among which they sang this angelical hymn, with
the Angels in Heaven." We are quite sure, therefore, that in very early times, the Angels' song was
enlarged into something like its present form, and
used in the Eastern Church, as a morning hymn.
Its Eucharistic use is Western. The heavenly song
comes, in our Prayer Book, just at the climax of
the Divine Service, when our hearts are filled with
love to Christ, and men's words seem insufficient
to express our feelings. Thus, having received
Angels' food, we sing Angels' words, in a burst of
thanksgiving.

Other fragments of early Christian hymns are
supposed to exist in the Bible, and may be found
in these passages : Acts iv. 24—30 ; Eph. v. 14 ;
I Tim. iii. 16 ; 2 Tim. ii. 11—13 ; Rev. i. 4—8 ; xi.
15—19 ; xv. 3, 4 ; xxi. 1—8 ; xxii. 10—18. Perhaps
some of these may have been the hymns sung by
Paul and Silas, when the prisoners heard them.

There is one word very largely used in the Bible
which, though we can hardly call it a hymn in
itself, must be spoken of in connection with hymns
—*Alleluia*, or, more properly, *Hallelu-jah*—" Praise
Jehovah," or " Praise the Lord." It occurs before
many of the Psalms (see Ps. civ. 35 ; cv. 45ʼ; cxlvi.,
cl., etc.), and was always sung by the Jews on solemn
days of rejoicing. It is supposed to be one of the
oldest words of devotion—for it has been found to
be used by many other nations. Perhaps, indeed,
it came straight from Heaven to earth, for S. John
(Rev. xix. 1—6) tells us how the heavenly host sang
" Alleluia." It became the " burden and prelude "

of all Christian song. Little children lisped it from their cradles, and by the fourth century it was known as the Christian shout of joy or victory. Christian rowers, as they rowed their boats, chanted Alleluia, as a song to make them pull together; and labourers at the plough sang it as they worked. This was not, however, in the earliest ages of the Church, for at first the Christians were very careful how they used it, fearing lest the angelic word might become a mere empty sound. S. Jerome tells us that the sound of the Alleluia summoned the monks to say their office; and we find, by his epitaph on Fabiola, that it was used at funerals. He says that "the whole multitude were singing psalms together, and making the golden roof of the church shake with echoing forth the Alleluia." One of our beautiful hymns for the burial of a child, translated from the Latin, retains the Alleluia :

> " Let no tears to-day be shed,
> Holy is this narrow bed.   Alleluia ! "
>   (Ch. Hy., 248.)

It was also much used at baptisms. The story of the Hallelujah Victory takes us back to the time when there were many Christians in Wales, but few in any other part of Britain, and there were numbers of heathen Picts and others, who robbed and plundered the country, and waged war against the Christians. S. Germanus had come over to preach in Britain against a certain heresy, and he converted and baptized a large number of people.

"The holy days of Lent were also at hand, and were rendered more religious by the presence of the priests, insomuch that the people, being instructed by daily sermons,

resorted in crowds to be baptized, for most of the army
desired admission to the saving water; a church was prepared with boughs for the feast of the resurrection of our
Lord, and so fitted up in that martial camp as if it were a
city. The army advanced, still wet with the baptismal
water, the faith of the people was strengthened, and whereas
human power had before been despaired of, the Divine
assistance was now relied upon. . . . A multitude of fierce
enemies appeared, whom as soon as those that lay in ambush
saw approaching, Germanus, bearing in his hands the
standard, instructed his men all in a loud voice to repeat his
words, and the enemy advancing securely, as thinking to
take them by surprise, the priests three times cried 'Hallelujah.' A universal shout of the same word followed, and
the hills resounding the echo on all sides, the enemy was
struck with dread, fearing that not only the neighbouring
rocks, but even the very skies were falling upon them ; and
such was their terror that their feet were not swift enough to
deliver them from it. They fled in disorder, casting away
their arms, and well satisfied if, with their naked bodies,
they could escape the danger ; many of them, in their pre-
cipitate and hasty flight, were swallowed up by the river
which they were passing. . . . The prelates thus triumphed
over the enemy without bloodshed, and gained a victory by
faith, without the aid of human force, and prepared to return
home."

Before we go on to study further the history of
hymns, we must remember the words of S. Paul,
which occur *twice* in his Epistles : " Speaking to
yourselves in psalms and hymns and spiritual
songs, singing and making melody *in your hearts*
to the Lord." Our hymns will be of no use to us
unless we *think* of the words as we sing them, and
"lift up our hearts" in praise and prayer. This
lesson is beautifully brought out in the curious old
"legend of the Magnificat." There was a certain
abbey, built on very marshy ground, and the monks
who lived in it led pure and holy lives, tending the

sick and sorrowing. But they had one great trouble, not one of them could sing. They tried to sing their Magnificat each day, though with harsh and croaky voices, yet with all their hearts. One day there came to the abbey a monk who had a lovely voice, and while he sang the others were silent, and that night the abbot had a dream. An angel appeared to him and asked him, " Why was Magnificat not sung to-night? All these years the voices of praise reached heaven, to-night there was silence." And then the abbot knew that the monk with the lovely voice was singing for earth and not for heaven, and that the other voices which had been silenced were more pleasing to God, though harsh and untunable, because the melody in them came *from the heart.*

II.

PRAYER-BOOK HYMNS.

" It was the custom of these Christians to meet on a fixed day, before light, and to sing together, in turn, a hymn to Christ as God, then to separate, and after a time re-assemble, in order to eat together a simple and harmless meal."—*Pliny's Letters.*

WE have spoken of the *canticles,* or Bible Songs, and we come now to what may be more strictly termed a *hymn,* and has, indeed, been called the *greatest of all hymns*—the Te Deum. It is said by tradition to have been composed by S. Ambrose, and sung in the Church at Milan at the baptism

B

of S. Augustine, the two saints answering each other in alternate verses, and Monica crying, "I had rather have thee, Augustinus, *Christian*, than Augustinus *Emperor.*"

But this legend, beautiful as it is, has no foundation, for we cannot trace the Te Deum, as it now stands, so far back in history. Its origin lies in obscurity, though the first ten verses, as we noticed before, existed in Greek in comparatively early times, and as a Latin hymn in its present, or nearly its present, form, it is known to have been used as a hymn for matins on Sunday, before the last lesson, from the beginning of the sixth century.

In different churches its form varies, but the last verses are always sentences taken mainly from the Bible, seven of them being from the Psalter and one from the Book of Daniel. The hymn is an act of adoration, beginning with praise from ourselves, and finally leads up to the song of the highest ranks of angels, using the very words of their worship, "Holy! Holy! Holy!" Then comes the adoration of the elect in Paradise—Apostles, Prophets, Martyrs, the Church triumphant uniting with the Church militant in the worship of the Holy Trinity.

Then the hymn is addressed to Christ, and becomes a kind of *creed*, of six verses, describing the Incarnation, the Redemption, the Resurrection, Ascension, and the glorious coming.

The third part of the hymn (verse 20 to end) is *prayer*, and in some churches, chiefly on the Continent, it is the custom for the people to kneel during the singing of it. Thus this most beautiful and " most famous non-biblical hymn of the early

Church " is a type of what every good hymn should be, an act of *praise*, of *faith*, and of *prayer*.

The Te Deum has been sung, not only at great religious festivals—Councils of the Church, coronations, public thanksgivings, baptisms, weddings— but on the battle-field, on the scaffold, on the occasion of great discoveries, as when Columbus and his crew discovered the New World, and when the first French adventurers reached the mouth of the Mississippi. Many of our greatest musicians have composed solemn Te Deums, and its history might form a book in itself.

Another very short " Prayer-book hymn " is the Gloria Patri, or lesser doxology, so called in contrast to the Gloria in Excelsis, or greater doxology, the "Glory be to the Father," etc., which we sing at the end of every Psalm. This dates, possibly, from the time of the Apostles, though the words, " As it was in the beginning," were added later, to confute some heretics who denied the eternal Deity of the Son of God. The Gloria Patri was offered as a solemn act of praise to God, not only after every Psalm—in the Western Church—or after the last Psalm in a section—in the Eastern Church—but also after many prayers, and, as we still keep it, under varying forms, after sermons. It is not only an act of praise, but a short creed in itself. Polycarp, one of the early Christian martyrs, used it when bound to the stake, before the flames reached him ; and Bede, a very saintly man, and a hymn-writer himself, died with the words of the Gloria upon his lips. In later days, *metrical* doxologies came into vogue, and were much used in Latin, and afterwards in English, our most famous one being Bishop Ken's—

"Praise God, from Whom all blessings flow,
Praise Him all creatures here below," etc.

Some of the old Latin doxologies are very beautiful, and emphasize the day or the season for which
they are appointed.

Another hymn used in our Liturgy, or Holy
Communion Office, besides the Gloria in Excelsis,
is the Tersanctus, also an angelic hymn, " Holy,
Holy, Holy, Lord God of hosts, heaven and earth
are full of Thy glory: Glory be to Thee, O Lord
most high " (see Isaiah vi. 3 ; Rev. iv. 8).   This
is taken directly from Holy Scripture, as also are
the other two Eucharistic hymns, which, though
not appointed to be used in our Prayer-book, are
now commonly employed as other hymns are—
the Benedictus and the Agnus Dei.   The first of
these is the triumphal chorus sung by the people as
they waved their palm-branches before our Blessed
Lord, on His entry into Jerusalem (S. Matt. xxi.
9 ; S. Mark xi. 9 ; S. Luke xix. 38).   The words
vary a little in the three Gospels ; S. Luke alone
giving us the angelic words, " Peace in heaven, glory
in the highest" (see S. Luke ii. 14, where the
words at the Saviour's birth are " peace on earth").
Geikie, in his *Life of Christ*, tells us that this was
sung, in the early Church, as one of the first
Christian hymns ; it would run something like
this—

"Hosanna to the Son of David,
Blessed is He that cometh in the Name of the Lord,
Peace in heaven, glory in the highest.
Blessed be the kingdom of our Father David,
That cometh in the Name of the Lord.
Hosanna in the highest."

It is always interesting to find our worship connected with the Temple worship, and we find that the words of the hymn are taken partly from Ps. cxviii. 25, 26, Bible version. *Hosanna*, " Save now," was a favourite Jewish cry, and we keep it in the versicle, " O Lord, save Thy people." The Benedictus is used sometimes in the most solemn part of our Liturgy—before the prayer of Consecration, and the Agnus Dei after it. The words of the latter hymn are also taken directly from the Bible (see S. John i. 29 ; S. Matt. viii. 8).

" O Lamb of God, that taketh away the sins of the world —have mercy upon us—grant us Thy peace."

The fragments of two old hymns are in our Burial Service, the *Media vita*, " In the midst of life we are in death," a very famous Latin hymn of the ninth century, written by Notker, a German monk, of whom we shall hear later, into which is woven the *Trisagion*, a much older hymn, which was used in the Liturgy, and has been sometimes confounded with the Tersanctus,—" Holy God, Holy and Mighty, Holy and Immortal, have mercy upon us." There is a legend that, at the time of a dreadful earthquake in Constantinople, about A.D. 434, this hymn was miraculously given from heaven to the terror-stricken people, but no doubt it is far older than that time.

The only *metrical* hymns left in our Prayer-book are two translations of the *Veni Creator*, a Latin hymn of the ninth century, which ranks only second to the Te Deum in fame, and has been used at Ordinations for many centuries. Of this hymn we shall speak later.

It is necessary that we should know the meaning of some of the words used in the Liturgy, and the first we will take is the word Anthem, which is derived from *Antiphon*, the alternate singing of a choir from side to side. This had its origin in the Jewish Church (1 Chron. vi. 31), and many of the Psalms, notably Psalm cxviii., were written to be sung *antiphonally*, that is, in turn.

This mode of singing was introduced into the Christian Church in its earliest ages. S. Ignatius of Antioch is said to have had a vision of angels in heaven singing antiphonally the praises of God, but it was used first in the Eastern Church, and may have arisen partly from the side to side singing of the Greek chorus. S. Basil tells us that, in his time, the Christians, " rising from their prayers, proceeded to singing of psalms, dividing themselves into two parts, and singing by turns." By degrees, the verses of psalms or hymns thus sung began to be called *antiphons*, and varied for different seasons.

The " Reproaches " or antiphons for Good Friday, " O my people, what have I done unto thee, wherein have I wearied thee ? Answer Me," were based on portions of Jer. ii. and Micah vi., and the *Trisagion* was woven in among them. They are still used in some of our churches in their prose form, and one metrical version has been made. Then there were the special antiphons to the Magnificat, sung on the eight days before Christmas, from which the several days took their name—for instance, we shall find December 16th in the Prayer-book calendar called *O Sapientia ;* the others being *O Adonai, O Root of Jesse, O Key of*

David, O Dawning Light, O King—desire of all nations, and *O Emmanuel*. Upon these the old hymn, *O come, O come, Emmanuel*, is founded.

Books, services, and seasons, as well as days, were sometimes named after antiphons. Thus Vespers for the Dead were called *Placebo*, from the antiphon to the first psalm; and matins for the dead, *Dirige*, for the same reason. The first Sunday in Lent was called *Invocavit me*, from the opening words of the Introit.

We only keep a few antiphons in our Prayer-book, the best known being that in the Burial Service, "I heard a voice from heaven," etc.; and that in the Visitation of the Sick, "O Saviour of the world, Who by Thy Cross and precious Blood hast redeemed us, save us and help us, we humbly beseech Thee, O Lord." The modern anthem grew out of the antiphon, and dates as part of the English service from 1662. An *Introit* was a short anthem, so called because sung when the faithful were entering the church. It is now sung at the beginning of the Holy Communion, as the clergy enter the altar rails. Some Sundays take their names from the special Introit for the day—the fourth Sunday in Lent, for instance, being called Lætare Sunday.

The *Gradual* was an anthem sung after the Epistle, and so called because chanted on the *steps* (gradus) as the deacon went up to the ambon, or altar. When sung by one person, it was called *Tractus*, or Tract.

The Alleluia, which afterwards grew into what was called the Sequence hymn, followed the Gradual. In our next chapter we shall come to

the earliest metrical hymns, having laid the foundation of our history upon the two great rocks—the
Bible and the Prayer-book.

III.

HYMNS OF THE EASTERN CHURCH.

SECOND TO SIXTH CENTURIES.

" Then it was first instituted that, after the manner of the
Eastern Churches, Hymns and Psalms should be sung."—
S. AUGUSTINE.

WE come now to the earliest metrical hymns,
which were written in Greek, and two *very* early
ones have been preserved to us.   The first was a
hymn for the young, by Clement of Alexandria,
composed between the years A.D. 190 and 195.   He
was a famous scholar and teacher, and the head of
a Christian school at Alexandria.   A persecution
broke out there, and he had to fly for his life.   The
hymn was found at the end of one of his books, a
Greek work, called *The Tutor.*   Many translations
have been made from it, but it is rugged and
not easy to render in English.   A free translation
is given in the Church Sunday School Hymn-
book—

" Shepherd of tender youth,
Guiding in love and truth,
   Through devious ways ;
Christ, our triumphant King,
We come Thy name to sing,
And here our children bring,
   To sing Thy praise.

Thou art our Holy Lord,
The all-subduing Word,
 Healer of strife,
Thou didst Thyself abase,
That from sin's deep disgrace
Thou mightest save our race,
 And give us life." etc.

The next is also a very old hymn, and much better known. It may belong to the second century, but the author and date are uncertain. It was the earliest metrical evening hymn of the Christian community, and was sung when the lamps were brought in at dusk. S. Basil, who was born in the year 329, mentions the hymn as an old one, even in his days. He says about it—" It seemed good to our forefathers not to receive the gift of the evening light altogether in silence, but to give thanks immediately upon its appearance."

The hymn has had many translators. The version in A. & M. (No. 18) is by Keble—

" Hail, gladdening light, of His pure glory formed."

There is another in Church Hymns (No. 25)—

" O Brightness of the Eternal Father's face."

And another, well known to us by Sullivan's beautiful music, is in Longfellow's *Golden Legend*, the hymn sung by Elsie and the children in the forester's cottage—

" O gladsome light of the Father eternal."

We may picture to ourselves one of those early Christian households. The work of the day was over; fathers and brothers returned from their field labours or business in the city. The sun had set, and the deepening twilight spread over hill and plain. Then the eldest daughter of the house would enter, bearing in her hands a lamp, and as she appeared the whole family would stand, their eyes raised to heaven, singing—

> "Gladsome light
> Of the immortal Father,
>   Holy, blessed, Jesus Christ,
> Having come to sunset,
> Beholding the light of evening,
>   We praise
> Father, Son, and Holy Spirit." etc.

The lamp was taken as the symbol of Christ, and thus, as in many other ways, religion was brought by these primitive Christians into every act of daily life. Might we not copy them, in these practical, unpoetical, scientific days? An old English custom was kept up until the time of Charles II., that when the lights were brought in at nightfall, the people said, "God send us the light of heaven," but this beautiful old custom was dropped by the Puritans. Psalms were also much used as *lamp-lighting* songs.

We must leave the Greek hymns for a little while, and turn to those written in *Syriac*, a language very much like Hebrew, and still more like the language spoken by the common people in Palestine in the time of our Lord. In the north-east of Syria was the town of Edessa, where lived a heretic called Bardesanes. He was a great poet, and composed many beautiful hymns, containing his false doctrines. He set them to popular tunes, and they so caught the fancy of the people that even the children soon knew them by heart, and used to sing them at their play, and thus the heresy

was spread. But God raised up a good man to
fight against it—a monk named Ephrem, of Edessa.
He saw to his grief how the false doctrines of Bardesanes were spreading, and determined to fight
against the heretic with his own weapons. So he
composed a large number of sound doctrinal
hymns, and trained young girls to sing them in
chorus. They were so beautiful, that all the city
flocked to hear them, and they checked the progress of the heresy. Thus we see, in the very early
days of Christianity, what we shall find exemplified
in all ages of the Church, the immense power and
value of hymn-singing. Many of Ephrem's hymns
were for children, and have titles such as, *The
Children in Paradise*, etc. Here is a verse from
one of his Sunday hymns—

> " Glory to the glorious One,
>   Good and great, one God alone,
>   Who this day hath glorified,
>   First and best of all beside,
>   Making it for every clime,
>   Of all times the sweetest time."

A hymn of Syriac origin, for Holy Baptism, said
to be by Ephrem, is given in Church Hymns (221)—

> " Glad sight ! the Holy Church
>   Spreads forth her wings of love,
>   To welcome to her breast a child
>   Begotten from above."

Ephrem died about the year 381, and with his
dying breath he made the daughter of the governor
of Syria swear never again to be carried by slaves,
because " the neck of man should bear no yoke
but that of Christ." Other Syriac hymn-writers
followed him, and their hymns are still used in

the ancient churches of Mesopotamia, Syria, and Western Persia. There the Syriac language is still used in the Liturgy, just as Latin is used in the Western Church ; but as a *vernacular* (that is, a language of the people), it has given way to others. These Christians, in the early centuries, fell into grievous error, and we are now sending to them teachers to help them to understand the true faith. In Southern India, on the Malabar coast, and near Madras, are the so-called *Christians of St. Thomas*, who speak Tamil as their language, but still use Syriac prayers and hymns in their Liturgy, showing that they are descendants, probably, of Assyrian Christians, who came, centuries ago, from Western Asia, and settled there.

But we must return to the Greek hymns, and to the next great hymn-poet, S. Gregory Nazianzen (A.D. 326—389), one of the Fathers of the Eastern Church. He was the first who banished pagan plays from the stage at Constantinople, and introduced stories from the Bible in their place, these being the earliest *miracle* or *mystery* plays, of which we shall hear later. We use none of his hymns now, in a metrical form, although many have come down to us.

There are translations also in A. & M. of two early Greek hymns, of unknown authorship. The first is the beautiful morning hymn of the fifth century—

" Awaked from sleep, we fall " (No. 474) ;

and the other, for Lent, belongs to the sixth or seventh century—

" Fain would I, Lord of Grace." (No. 491.)

The last Greek hymn-writer we shall speak of in this chapter is S. Anatolius, who lived in the sixth or seventh century, and of whom we know very little. He is said to have been the author of a very celebrated hymn—the great evening hymn of the Greek Church—which comes in the *Great After Supper*, or *After Vespers* Service. It is a long hymn, and Dr. Neale translated some parts of it, and made it into our lovely evening hymn—

"The day is past and over." (Ch. Hy., 31 ; A. & M., 21.)

He says—" It is to the scattered hamlets of Chios and Mitylene what Bishop Ken's evening hymn is to the villages of our own land." Another translation by Dr. Neale from a hymn of Anatolius is to be found in the Hymnal Companion (534)—

> "Fierce was the wild billow,
>   Dark was the night,
> Oars laboured heavily,
>   Foam glittered white ;
> Trembled the mariner,
>   Peril was high,
> Then said the Son of God,
>   ' Peace !—It is I.' " etc.

We will finish this chapter by describing a scene, very similar to that at Edessa, where, no doubt, many of the Greek hymns we have spoken of were used. There was a famous heretic called Arius, who, like his forerunner, Bardesanes, made his doctrines popular by the hymns which he composed, and set to lively, taking tunes. The Arians had been forbidden to hold worship at Constantinople ; but when S. John Chrysostom arrived there as Bishop, he found that these heretics used to meet on Sundays and Festivals outside the city walls, and sing their hymns, after sunset, in procession through the streets. So he set up, like S. Ephrem, rival bands of *orthodox* hymn-singers, who carried crosses and lights, and formed nightly processions, often coming into contact with the Arians. But, unhappily, their rival singing caused so much rioting and bloodshed, that, after the chief officer of the Empress had been wounded, a stop was put to the processions. At Alexandria, Athanasius used the same means to fight against the doctrines of Arius, and thus, in three great centres of the Church, hymns were used almost, as we might say, as weapons in a religious warfare, and so became much more popular and more widely spread.

IV.

LATER GREEK HYMNS.

SEVENTH, EIGHTH, AND NINTH CENTURIES.

"Nothing so lifteth up and, as it were, wingeth the soul, so freeth it from earth and looseth it from the chains of the body, so leadeth it into wisdom and a contempt of all earthly things, as the choral symphony of a sacred hymn." —S. CHRYSOSTOM.

BEFORE telling the stories of the Greek hymns of the seventh, eighth, and ninth centuries, it will be necessary to describe the *form* in which they were written. The Eastern Liturgies contain many different forms, but the three with which we shall have most to do are the *Idiomelon*, the *Ode*, and the *Canon*. The first of these was much the same as any other short hymn, being sung at great Festivals, at Matins, and most of all during the quiet hours of the night, in the western part of the Church, "glowing with the processional torches." When several of these were combined, they were called *Stichera* (verses) or *Idiomela*.

The *Ode* was made up of a variable number of short strophes, or verses ; each of which had the highest expression of feeling thrown into the closing line. Odes are found in *groups ;* sometimes a pair, but more often a series of three, or of eight or nine, the latter number forming a Canon.

The *Canon* was the highest form of Greek hymnody, and was founded on the Canticles then used. There was a separate Canticle for each day of the week. *Monday*, the song of Moses (Ex. xv.) ; *Tuesday*, the song of Moses (Deut. xxxii.) ; *Wednesday*, the song of Hannah ; *Thursday*, the song of Habakkuk ; *Friday*, Isaiah xxvi. 9—20 ; *Saturday*, Jonah's Prayer ; *Sunday*, the first part of the Benedicite. To these seven were added (eight) the rest of the Benedicite ; (nine) the Magnificat and Benedictus. Thus the Canon, in its full form, consisted of nine odes, but the second Canticle is so severe and penitential in its character, that the ode corresponding to it is only found in Lenten Canons, so that most consist of eight odes only.

The great master of the Canon was S. Andrew of Crete (A.D. 663—732), who was born at Damascus, and became a monk at Jerusalem, and afterwards Archbishop of Crete. He wrote what is called the *Great Canon*, or King of Canons, for

Mid-Lent week, consisting of three hundred stanzas of examples from the Bible of penitential grief. The hymn—

> "Whence shall my tears begin?"

is taken from it. But S. Andrew's name will be memorable to us through Dr. Neale's grand rendering of the hymn taken from the Canon for the second week in Lent—

> "Christian, dost thou see them?"
>
> (Ch. Hy., 104 ; A. & M., 91.)

Next comes one who, in contrast with S. Andrew, we may call our *Easter* poet, S. John Damascene, also a native of Damascus. He was born of wealthy parents, about the beginning of the eighth century, and died A.D. 780. He is generally thought to be the *greatest* of the Greek hymn-poets. He retired from the world to the famous monastery of Mar Saba, built on the steep slopes of the Kedron Valley, near the Dead Sea, where his tomb is still shown. One of his most famous hymns was called *The Stichera of the Last Kiss.* - These were solemn verses, sung by the grave-side, in the funeral service of the Eastern Church, while friends and relations gave a parting kiss to the corpse, the priest kissing it last of all.

> "Take the last kiss, the last for ever,
>   Yet render thanks amid your gloom ;
>   He, severed from his home and kindred,
>   Is passing onwards to the tomb.
>   For earthly labours, earthly pleasures,
>   And carnal joys he cares no more ;
>   Where are his kinsfolk and acquaintance?
>   They stand upon another shore.
>   Let us say, around him pressed,
>   Grant him, Lord, ' eternal rest.'"

S. John also did much service to the *music* of the Eastern Church—training choristers, and, so some say, founding the system of notation. He wrote three great Canons for Easter Sunday, Low Sunday, and Ascension Day. The first was called the *Golden Canon*, or Queen of Canons, and is the grandest piece in Greek sacred poetry. Our beautiful Easter hymn, translated by Dr. Neale,

"The Day of Resurrection" (Ch. Hy., 137 ; A. & M., 132),

is taken from the first ode of this great Canon, and the other Easter hymn we owe to S. John is from the Canon for Low Sunday—

"Come, ye faithful, raise the strain."
(Ch. Hy., 135 ; A. & M., 133.)

Dr. Neale has given us a description of an Easter Eve at Athens, thus—

"As midnight approached, the Archbishop, with his priests, accompanied by the King and Queen, left the church, and stationed themselves on the platform. Every one remained in breathless expectation, holding their unlighted tapers in readiness when the glad moment should come. Suddenly, the single report of a cannon announced that twelve had struck, and Easter Day begun. The Archbishop, raising the cross, exclaimed, 'Christ is risen,' and every one took up the cry. The darkness was succeeded by a blaze of light from the tapers, and bands of music struck up joyous strains. The drum rolled through the town, the cannon roared, rockets flashed up hill and plain. Men clasped each other's hands, and the aged priest chanted a glorious old hymn of victory."

This was a short hymn—

"Christ is risen from the dead,
Death by death down doth He tread,
And on those within the tombs
He bestoweth life."

C

After this had been repeated two or three times, the *Golden Canon* of S. John was sung.

Another hymn we owe to him is taken from an Idiomela for All Saints ; it is very beautiful—

> " Those eternal bowers man hath never trod."
>
> (Ch. Hy., 524.)

We come back to the monastery of Mar Saba for two more hymn-poets—one the foster-brother, the other the nephew of S. John Damascene. *S. Cosmas* holds the second place among the Greek ecclesiastical poets. He and S. John were brothers in friendship and in love, and excited one another to write hymns. S. Cosmas was very fond of *types :* he wrote two fine canons for Christmas Day and for the Transfiguration. From the first a hymn (No. 142, Hymnary) is taken—

> " Christ is born, tell forth His fame,
> Christ from heaven, His love proclaim ;
> Christ on earth, exalt His name !
> Sing to the Lord, O world, with exultation,
> Break forth in glad thanksgiving, every nation,
> For He hath triumphed gloriously."

From the second, a beautiful Transfiguration hymn—

> " In days of old, on Sinai." (No. 460, A. & M.)

The last and youngest of the trio of the hymn-writers of Mar Saba was S. Stephen the Sabaite (A.D. 725—794). He entered the monastery at the early age of ten—perhaps because he was the nephew of the great doctor—and spent the whole of his life there, dying in his seventieth year. From one of his hymns Dr. Neale (if he did not quite translate it) took the idea of

"Art thou weary, art thou languid?"
(Ch. Hy., 333 ; A. & M., 254.)

It seems to picture to us the wilderness in which Mar Saba was placed, with the glimpse of the Dead Sea, through which Jordan flowed, and to convey the feeling of languor and weariness which no doubt the monks often experienced.

S. Stephen also wrote a fine poem called *The Martyrs of Mar Saba*, giving an account of monks killed in defending their monastery from robbers.

There was another great religious house in the East, which also became the home of hymn-writers : this was the monastery of the *Studium*, at Constantinople, where dwelt the poets S. Theodore, S. Theophanes, and S. Joseph. Theodore (*d.* 826) wrote a grand Canon on the Judgment, said to be the finest before the *Dies Iræ* was composed. Theophanes was a fine poet, but we have few English translations from his works. But to Joseph of the Studium, the last Greek hymn-poet we shall name, we owe some very favourite hymns. He lived in the early part of the ninth century, and was a native of Sicily. He was captured by pirates, and became a slave in Crete, but, after regaining his liberty, he went to Constantinople and became a monk of the Studium. No doubt he had seen much of sailors and seafaring life, and understood their trials and dangers, for he gave us the beautiful hymn—

"Safe home, safe home in port."
(Ch. Hy., 462 ; A. & M., 609.)

Dr. Neale, to whom we owe nearly all our best translations of Greek hymns, had this sung to him

on his death-bed.   Other hymns founded on those
of S. Joseph are—

> "Stars of the morning, all gloriously bright."
> (Ch. Hy., 186 ; A. & M., 423.)
> "O happy band of pilgrims."
> (Ch. Hy., 468 ; A. & M., 224.)
> "Let our choir new anthems raise."
> (Ch. Hy., 200 ; A. & M., 423.)

This last Saint's Day hymn is taken from a long
Canon for the feast of SS. Timothy and Maura, a
deacon of Constantinople and his wife, who suffered
martyrdom, A.D. 304.   Kingsley has written a
beautiful poem on the subject, called *S. Maura.*
The story tells how Maura at first wished her
husband to deny Christ to save himself, but when
she saw his reproachful look she repented, and
asked to be crucified by his side.   As they hung
upon two crosses, close together, suffering torture
for Christ's sake, Timothy preached to the people
from the cross, and his wife encouraged him, until
death put an end to their sufferings.

We must leave our beautiful Greek hymns now,
although we might learn much more about them,
hoping that, before very long, a second Dr. Neale
may arise, and more may be translated for us.
From the year 900 they gradually declined, and .
gave way to the large influx of Latin hymns. Two
verses from S. Joseph's *Canon on the Ascension,*
said to be the finest Ascension hymn extant, will
conclude our chapter—

> "Jesus, Lord of life eternal,
> Taking those He loved the best,
> Stood upon the Mount of Olives,
> And His own the last time blest ;

Then, though He had never left it,
Sought again His Father's Breast.

Knit is now our flesh to Godhead,
Knit in everlasting bonds ;
Call the world to highest festal,
Floods and oceans, clap your hands ;
Angels, raise the song of triumph,
Make response, ye distant lands."
(Sarum Hymnal, 101.)

V.

LATIN HYMNS OF FOURTH AND FIFTH CENTURIES.

AMBROSIAN.

" How did I weep, in Thy hymns and canticles, touched to the quick by the voices of Thy sweet attuned Church. The voices flowed into mine ears, and the Truth distilled into my heart ; whence the affection of my devotion overflowed, and tears ran down, and happy was I therein."— S. AUGUSTINE.

WE must turn back now for awhile to the Western Church, and see what her hymn-writers were doing all this time.

The first Latin hymn-poet of whom we know anything was S. Hilary of Poitiers. In our Prayer-book calendar, January 13th is dedicated to him. He died in January 368. His morning hymn is the best known—

" Thou bounteous Giver of the light."

But the real founder of hymn-singing in the West was S. Ambrose (340—397), perhaps the

greatest bishop the world has ever seen. He was
born at Tréves, and was the son of a prefect in
Gaul. The story is told that, when an infant in
the cradle, a swarm of bees lighted upon his head
and mouth, without injuring him, and that his
father, on seeing this, exclaimed, " If the boy lives
he will be a great man." For this reason the old
pictures represent him with a beehive near him.

Ambrose was highly educated in Rome, where
his mother removed after her husband's death, but
was brought up a heathen. He was appointed
Governor of Liguria and Prefect of Milan. The
Bishop of that place died, and there was a quarrel
between Catholics and Arians who should be
Bishop. Ambrose appeared to quell the disturb-
ance, and as he spoke to the people, they listening
in silence, a child's voice was heard saying,
"Ambrose shall be Bishop!" The people took up
the cry and forced him to consent. He tried to
fly, declaring that though a Christian by conviction,
he had never been baptized; but the Emperor
commanded him to consent, and within eight days
he was baptized, ordained, and consecrated. The
Empress Justinia had made a demand that one
church in Milan should be given up for Arian
worship. Ambrose refused, and soldiers were sent
to try and force the church from him. The people
were so devoted to their Bishop that they stuck to
him and kept guard day and night in the church,
ready, if need be, to die with him. He preached
to them, and gave them hymns to sing—in some
cases with tunes of his own—so as to cheer their
spirits. S. Augustine tells us the story, and these
are his own words about it—

" At this time it was instituted that, after the manner of the Eastern Churches, hymns and psalms should be sung, lest the people should grow weary and faint through their sorrow ; which custom has ever since been retained, and is cultivated by almost all the congregations throughout the world."

So that grand old church at Milan was the nursery of our Western hymn-singing. The soldiers watched the church all day and night, and at last, finding Ambrose determined, they left ; probably being all really in favour of him. Monica was in the congregation, for S. Augustine says—

" The devout people kept watch in the church ready to die with their Bishop, Thy servant. There my mother, Thy handmaid, bearing a chief part of those anxieties and watchings, lived for prayer."

There are nearly one hundred hymns extant called Ambrosian, some of which were written by the good Bishop himself, and some which belong to the period in which he lived. Four of them are quoted by Augustine, His mother, Monica, to whom he was devoted, died some time after he had become a Christian. The night after her funeral, as he lay upon his bed stricken with grief, he says—

" Then I slept, and woke up again, and found my grief not a little softened ; and as I was alone in my bed I remembered those true verses of Ambrose—

' Maker of all, the Lord,
    And Ruler of the height,
Who, robing day in light, has poured
    Soft slumbers o'er the night,
That to our limbs the power
    Of toil may be renewed,
And hearts be raised that sink and cower,
    And sorrows be subdued.' "

The grand Advent hymn, given in A. & M. (55) among the hymns for Christmas—

> "O come, Redeemer of mankind, appear,"

is, perhaps, the noblest hymn of S. Ambrose, full, as indeed they all are, of sound doctrine and faith. He had a way of making things very clear, and wrote to uphold the true teaching of the Church against Arianism. Here we have emphasized the great doctrine of the Incarnation—

> "Of twofold substance, human and Divine,
> As giant swift, rejoicing on His way."

To S. Ambrose we owe, also, the beautiful little evening hymn, *O lux beata Trinitas*—

> "O Trinity, most blessed light" (A. & M., 14),

on which is founded the better known

> "Three in One, and One in Three"
> (Ch. Hy., 529 ; A. & M., 163),

taken probably from a German version of the Latin. Thus from Latin to German, from German back to English, the main idea of the hymn is kept, and its beauty cannot die. Two versions of another of his hymns are given in A. & M., the *Aeterna Christi munera*, and a hymn for martyrs.

> "The eternal gifts of Christ the King." (No. 430.)
> "Ye servants of our glorious King." (No. 444.)

And two beautiful morning hymns are also ascribed to him, the first being the hymn sung for 1600 years at the hour of prime—

> "Now that the daylight fills the sky."
> (Ch. Hy., 9 ; A. & M., 1.)

The second, the beautiful hymn to the Holy Trinity, especially to Christ, the Light of the

world, and a prayer for help and guidance through
the day—

· "O Jesu, Lord of life and grace."
(Ch. Hy., 11 ; A. & M., 2.)

This is one of his creed-like hymns, describing the
true faith of the writer. Those who are troubled
with doubts and difficulties cannot do better than
turn to these fine hymns of the early Church, which
have lasted more than fifteen centuries, and still
remain as fresh and beautiful as ever.

S. Ambrose, too, introduced the grander form of
worship. He divided the singers into two choirs,
singing chants and alternate responses. His
music, like his poetry, was severe, but more
melodious than that of Gregory, and a great im-
provement on any Church music that had hitherto
been used. Before giving a list of some of the
best known Ambrosian hymns now in use, we must
give a little time to one of the most celebrated,
said, though without good authority, to be by S.
Ambrose himself, and at any rate belonging to his
time—

"At the Lamb's high feast we sing."
(Ch. Hy., 128 ; A. & M , 127.)

A second translation of this hymn is given in
A. & M.—

"The Lamb's high banquet called to share." (No. 128.)

Dr. Neale says—"In order to understand this hymn, we
must know for whom it was written. It was the custom of
the early Church that baptism should be administered to
Catechumens on Easter Eve. A white garment was given
to each of the persons baptized, with words like these, 'Take
this white vesture, for a token of the innocence which by
God's grace, in this Holy Sacrament of Baptism, is given
unto thee, and for a sign whereby thou art admonished, as

long as thou livest, to give thyself to innocency of living,
that after this transitory life thou mayest be partaker of life
everlasting.'"

The *chrisom* robes, as they were called, were worn
from Easter Eve to Low Sunday, and for this
reason the week-days were marked *in albis*—" in
white." So that the second line of the hymn
refers to the snow-white chrisom robes—

"Arrayed in garments white and fair."

And the banquet they were waiting for was the
Holy Communion. Thus the study of these old
hymns teaches us the history and customs of the
early Church. The Ambrosian hymns are very
numerous, and these are only a few of the best
known—

"Come, Holy Ghost, Who ever one."
(Ch. Hy., 347 ; A. & M., 9.)
" O God, of all the Strength and Power."
(A. & M., 11.)
" O Strength and Stay, upholding all creation."
(Ch. Hy., 15 ; A. & M., 12.)
" Before the ending of the day."
(Ch. Hy., 19 ; A. & M., 15.)
" Hark, a thrilling voice is sounding."
(Ch. Hy., 67 ; A. & M., 47.)
" O Christ, Who art the light and day."
(A. & M., 95.)
" Light's glittering morn bedecks the sky."
(A. & M., 126 ; Parts 1, 2, 3.)
" Jesu, our hope, our heart's desire."
(A. & M., 150.)

The next great Latin hymn-poet was *Prudentius*
(348—413). He was born in Spain, and was a
lawyer and judge, holding a high appointment at
court. When about fifty-seven years old, a change

came over him ; he felt that worldly fame could not satisfy him, and determined to devote the rest of his life to God. At this time he wrote his hymns. Two are still great favourites ; the Epiphany one—

"Earth has many a noble city" (A. & M., 76),

and the lovely little hymn for Holy Innocents' Day—

"Sweet flowrets of the martyr band." (A. & M., 68.)

He also wrote a long Christmas poem, from which is taken our Christmas hymn—

"Of the Father's love begotten" (A. & M., 56),

with its refrain, "evermore and evermore"; and a good hymn for Sunday evening—

"Father most high, be with us." (A. & M., 493.)

VI.

LATIN HYMNS OF SIXTH AND SEVENTH CENTURIES.

GREGORY AND FORTUNATUS.

"The singing of psalms bringeth with it much gain, support, and sanctification, and can supply various lessons of wisdom, if the words purify the heart and the Holy Ghost straightway descends on the soul of the singer."—S. CHRYSOSTOM.

WE pass on to the sixth century, and to a name second only to S. Ambrose, *Gregory the Great.*

He was born at Rome, in the year 540, and was
the son of a rich Roman senator, sprung from one
of the most illustrious Roman races.   His mother,
Sylvia, was a very clever woman, and taught her
son well.   He became prætor of Rome, and the
people were very fond of him.   Then he made a
friendship with the followers of S. Benedict, and
broke all worldly ties, devoting his money to the
foundation of six new monasteries in Sicily.   In
his own palace, on the Cœlian Hill in Rome, he
founded a seventh, under the rule of S. Benedict,
and himself became a monk there.   He distributed
all the rest of his wealth to the poor and served the
beggars with his own hands, in his own house.
He was soon made one of the cardinal deacons of
Rome, and then sent, as Nuncio, to the Emperor
Tiberius, at Constantinople.   Then he returned to
Rome, to his peaceful monastery, of which he was
elected abbot, being much loved by all the monks.
Every one knows the story of the angel children in
the market-place, and how Gregory set off on his
way to England, but was brought back again by the
Pope's messenger, for the people could not spare him
from Rome.   In the year 390 he was elected Pope ;
at first he refused and fled from the city, wandering for days in disguise in the woods, but he was
discovered and led back to reign.   It was to the
Liturgy, or service of the Church, that Gregory gave
the most help.   He collected the ancient melodies
of the Church, and arranged them for worship.   He
also composed the words and music of several
hymns, and established at Rome a celebrated school
of religious music, where Christians of every nation
came to learn.   The little room in Rome is still to

be seen where he taught the choristers singing, and the whip which he is said to have used to correct them.

When the missionaries were sent to England, Gregory did not forget what music could do to help on the work of the mission. S. Augustine brought with him, from Rome, a band of trained choristers, and Ethelbert and Bertha were much impressed by their singing and solemn chanting. No doubt, besides the older hymns of S. Ambrose and others, they would sing some of those written by Gregory himself. These are some which have been ascribed to him :—

1. Sunday morning. "On this day, when days began." ✓
   (Ch. Hy., 37.)

2. Sunday evening. "Blest Creator of the light."
   (A. & M., 38.)

3. Lent. "Good it is to keep the fast." (A. & M., 89.)

4. Lent. "O merciful Creator, hear." (A. & M., 87 ;
   Ch. Hy., 109.)

5. Lent. "Lo ! now is our accepted day." (A. & M., 88.)

6. Lent. "O Thou Who dost to man accord."
   (A. & M., 86.)

7. And two hymns for early morning, translated by Cardinal Newman.

Gregory was the first Pope who took the title of "Servant of the servants of God," and he acted up to the title by having twelve poor pilgrims to dine with him every day, serving them, and washing their hands and feet. He also sent dishes to the sick from his own table. Gregory is generally represented in pictures with a dove, the legend being that his secretary once saw the Holy

Ghost, in the form of a dove, perched upon his shoulder while he was writing. He wrote much on the books of the Bible, and ranks with S. Ambrose, S. Augustine, and S. Jerome, among the four Fathers of the Latin Church. He died March 12, 604, aged 55.

Another Bishop of Poitiers, who lived two centuries or more after S. Hilary, wrote some famous hymns. His name was Venantius Fortunatus, and he was an Italian by birth, and passed his early life as a wandering minstrel, earning money by his clever verse. His youth was spent in gaiety, and when a student at Ravenna he became nearly blind, and recovered his sight, miraculously, as he thought, after anointing his eyes with oil taken from a lamp that burned upon the altar tomb of S. Martin at Tours ; so he made a pilgrimage to that place, and from that time led a changed life. He was always a great favourite, from his wit and gay humour, and after he became a monk was able to turn to use for the Church his valuable gift of poesy.

There was a certain princess, by name Rhadegund, a daughter of the King of Thuringia, who was made prisoner by Clotaire I. in 529. He made her his wife, but she had such a longing to take the veil, that at last her husband let her do so, and gave her permission to found a monastery at Poitiers. She led a most saintly life, preferring to be a simple nun, while a young girl took the place of Abbess. The climax of her happiness was reached when the Emperor Justin granted her a fragment of the true Cross, as a sacred relic for her monastery. Fortunatus was at that time visiting the sanctuaries of Southern France, and had formed

a friendship with S. Rhadegund. He wrote his
famous hymn *Vexilla Regis,*

"The Royal banners forward go."
(Ch. Hy., 118; A. & M., 96),

for the reception of this part of the true Cross at
Poitiers. It is a grand processional hymn, and
this is a description of the way it was sung—

"Escorted by a numerous body of clergy, and of the faithful, holding lighted torches, the Bishop started in the midst
of liturgical chants, which ceased not to resound in honour of
the hallowed wood of the Redemption. A league from
Poitiers, the pious cortége found the delegates of Rhadegund
—Fortunatus at their head—rejoicing in the honour which
had fallen to them; some carrying censers with perfumed
incense, others torches of white wax. The meeting took
place at Migné, at the place where, twelve centuries and a
half later, the cross appeared in the air. It was on this
occasion that the hymn *Vexilla Regis* was heard for the
first time—the chant of triumph, composed by Fortunatus,
to salute the arrival of the true Cross. It was the 19th
November, 569."

We can picture the grandeur and solemnity of
the scene, as they chanted—

"O Tree of glory, Tree most fair,
Ordained those Holy limbs to bear;
How bright in purple robe it stood,
The purple of a Saviour's blood."

Fortunatus used, in this hymn, the word *pati-
bulum*,[1] which means a cross formed thus—Y, or
thus ψ; this last form representing the stem of the
tree, with the branches on which, as on a balance,
the ransom of the world was weighed (ver. 5).

"Upon its arms, like balance true,
He weighed the price for sinners due."

---

[1] See *Dictionary of Hymnology*, p. 1220.

The hymn has always been sung on Passion Sunday, and also as a daily hymn from that time to Maundy Thursday. Our other equally famous Passion Sunday hymn, the *Pange lingua Gloriosi*,

> "Sing, my soul, the glorious battle"
> (Ch. Hy., 117 ; A. & M., 97),

was also written by Fortunatus, for the Abbey of St. Croix, on the same subject. The second verse refers, no doubt, to the ancient mediæval legend that the Cross of Christ was made from part of a tree which sprang from the seed of the Tree of Life—the seed being given to Adam or to Seth, by the angel who guarded the Garden of Eden, and that so God

> "Marked e'en then this tree, the ruin
> Of the first tree to dispel."

This hymn was used all through Lent, and most of all on Good Friday. Another of our Passion hymns, by Bishop Mant,

> "See the destined day arise" (A. & M. 113),

is also, most likely, taken from the *Pange lingua*. Fortunatus also composed a splendid Easter Processional—the *Salve Festa Dies*—said to have been sung by Jerome of Prague at the stake, A.D. 1416. He looked upon the day of his death as his birthday, and welcomed it as such, singing—

> "Hail, festal day, for evermore adored,
> Wherein God conquered Hell, and upward soared ;
>
> See the world's beauty, budding forth anew,
> Shows with the Lord, His gifts returning too.
>
> The earth with flowers is decked ; the sky serene,
> The heavenly portals glow with brighter sheen." etc.

We have another translation of the hymn—

"'Welcome, happy morning!' age to age shall say."
(Ch. Hy., 131 ; A. & M., 497.)

There is a similar Latin hymn for the Ascension, beginning in the same way, and no doubt founded on that of Fortunatus. He also wrote à hymn for the Annunciation—

"The God Whom earth, and sea, and sky." (A. & M., 449.)

·He was made Bishop in the year 599, twelve years after the death of Queen Rhadegund. He died in the year 609.

For the next two centuries we hear of no great names among Latin hymn-writers, but many beautiful hymns, whose authors' names are unknown, come down to us from this time. One is the "rugged but fine old hymn," *Urbs Beata Hierusalem*, "sung throughout Europe of old time," and said to belong to the seventh century. It is a splendid paraphrase of Rev. xxi. 2, 19, 21, and has been beautifully translated for us by Dr. Neale—

" Blessed city, Heavenly Salem."
" Christ is made the sure foundation."
(Ch. Hy., 338 ; A. & M., 396.)   Parts 1 & 2.

It is a grand description of the glories of the heavenly Jerusalem, and "a hymn of degrees," ascending from things earthly to things heavenly, and making the first interpreters of the last. The prevailing intention in building and dedicating a church with the rites thereto appertaining was to carry up men's thoughts from that temple built with hands, which they saw, to that other, built of

D

living stones in heaven, of which this was but a weak shadow.

Two Ascension Hymns (Nos. 144 and 145, A. & M.) also belong to this time.

VII.

LATIN HYMNS OF NINTH AND TENTH CENTURIES.

SEQUENCES.

" What, then, is more blessed than to imitate on the earth the concert of angels ; than to haste to prayer at the very dawn of day, and to honour the Creator with hymns and songs ; then, when the sun shines brightly, turning to work in which prayer is ever present, to spice our labours with hymns as with salt."—S. BASIL.

THERE is a story connected with the very favourite and well-known hymn for Palm Sunday—

> " All glory, laud, and honour
> To Thee, Redeemer, King."
> (Ch. Hy., 113 ; A. & M., 98).

At the beginning of the ninth century, there lived a good bishop, named Theodulph, who was unjustly imprisoned by the Emperor, in the town of Metz, or, as some say, Angers. On Palm Sunday there was a grand procession through the town ; the clergy and choristers, carrying palms blessed by the Pope, being followed by the Emperor himself. As they passed the prison walls, a voice was heard chanting a hymn of praise. The Emperor asked

to see the singer, and when Theodulph himself
appeared singing the new hymn he had composed
during his dreary imprisonment, he was pardoned
and set free. Such is said to be the origin of the
"All glory, laud, and honour," sung every Palm
Sunday through Christendom, for so many hundred
years, as a Processional hymn. There were many
different customs and ways of singing it. According to Sarum Use, the first four stanzas were sung
by seven boys, near the south door, before leaving
the church. In the York Use, the choir boys seem
to have gone up to a temporary gallery over the
church door, and there sung the first four stanzas.
After each of the first three stanzas, the choir,
kneeling below, sang the refrain ("All glory, laud,
and honour"). At the end of the fourth stanza the
boys began the refrain, and the rest of the choir,
standing up, sang it with them. In the Hereford
Use, the procession went to the gates of the town.
These being shut, seven boys of the choir went up
the tower, and there sang the refrain. In the Uses
of Tours and Rouen, the hymn was also sung at the
gates of the city.

About the same time (815) two fine hymns for
S. Michael and All Angels were composed by S.
Rhabanus Maurus. The translation of one is in
A. & M., 616—

"Life and strength of all Thy servants."

We now come to the celebrated *Sequence* Hymns,
which had their rise also in the ninth century.
There was a very famous religious house, called
the Abbey of S. Gall, near Constance, and there
lived a monk named Notker. He was struck with

the wearisomeness and almost vain repetition of the word *Alleluia* used in the Liturgy before the Gospel. The final syllable, *ia*, used to be sung over and over again, like a run, and it struck him what a good thing it would be to put words to the musical notes or sequences. So he wrote a hymn and took it to one of the two precentors of the Abbey Church, who, after suggesting some alterations, "gave thanks to God, and commended the new composition to the brethren of the monastery." This was the origin of the Sequence Hymns, sung between the Epistle and Gospel, and generally bearing upon the special festival or subject of the day. At first they were called *Proses*, because not written in a metrical form. Notker composed about thirty-five of these Sequence Hymns ; one, on the Holy Spirit, being especially beautiful. Tradition says that this was suggested to him by the sound of the mill-wheel turning. It soon became popular throughout Europe, and in a Spanish Missal the priest is ordered to hold a *white dove* in his hands, while intoning the first syllables of the hymn, and then to let it go, of course, as a symbol of the Holy Spirit. Notker left another beautiful legacy to the Church, in a hymn, or antiphon, called *Media vita*,[1] part of which is still kept in our Burial Service.

"In the midst of life we are in death : of whom may we seek for succour, but of Thee, O Lord, Who for our sins art justly displeased," etc.

Notker is said, according to the story, to have composed it while watching some workmen build

[1] See p. 95.

a bridge over a mountain gorge at peril of their lives ; or, as another tradition [1] says, while watching some boys climb the cliffs, near S. Gall, to gather samphire. By the middle of the thirteenth century this hymn had come into universal use as a supplication in time of trouble, and was even used as an incantation. It was supposed to be magic in its effects, and was also used at funerals and as a battle song.

The *Trisagion*, the very old Greek hymn of which we have heard, " Holy Lord," etc., is woven into it. Luther made a very good metrical translation of the *Media vita* into German, which is still much in use, for the dying, in his country. All Notker's hymns are very earnest and devout.

Another monk, named Godescalcus, who lived with Notker at the Abbey of S. Gall, is said to have written the famous Alleluiatic Sequence—

" The strain upraise of joy and praise."
(Ch. Hy., 516 ; A. & M., 295),

but it was more probably also by Notker. This was originally written for Epiphany, when the Alleluia was used for the last time before Easter.

Two other hymns to the Holy Spirit were probaby written about this time—the *Veni Creator*, and the *Veni sancte spiritus*. Both are said to have been composed by kingly hymn-writers—the first by Charlemagne, the second by King Robert II. of France, but we have no good authority for supposing this to be true.

The *Veni Creator*—" Come, Holy Ghost, our souls inspire "—holds the second place only to the Te

[1] It must be said that the evidence for these traditions is very uncertain.

Deum among the famous Latin hymns, and is the
only metrical hymn left in our Prayer-books, the
translation in the Ordination Service being, most
probably, by Bishop Cosin.   There is another
translation, by Caswall, in A. & M., 347—

> " Come, Holy Ghost, Creator Blest."

If this hymn could speak, it could tell us almost as
interesting a history as the Te Deum.   It has been
used for ten centuries throughout the Western
Church, not only at ordinations and consecrations
of bishops, but at the coronation of kings, at great
meetings and synods, and at confirmations.   In
medieval times, the singing of the *Veni Creator* was
marked by ringing of bells, use of incense, lights,
and the best vestments.   There is no evidence as
to its authorship.   It has been ascribed to Ambrose,
Gregory, and others.   It has not been found in
any MSS. earlier than the latter part of the tenth
century.   The *Veni sancte spiritus*—

> " Come, Thou Holy Spirit, come :
> And from Thy celestial home " (A. & M., 156),

" the loveliest of all the hymns in the whole circle
of Latin poetry," as Archbishop Trench calls it,
has been assigned to Stephen Langton, Archbishop
of Canterbury, and to Pope Innocent III., besides
King Robert.   It was called the Golden Sequence.
Robert II. was a good man, learned and accom-
plished, a musician and a poet, though a weak
king.   He directed the choir of the Church of S.
Denis, and used to sing with the monks at mass.
He certainly wrote other hymns, with suitable
music, and presented them at Rome on the Altar

of S. Peter. One of King Robert's friends, S. Fulbert, Bishop of Chartres, gave us the Easter hymn, *Chorus novæ Jerusalem*—

"Ye choirs of New Jerusalem" (A. & M., 125),

the second verse of which is founded on a curious old medieval belief that the lion's whelps are born dead, and their father, by roaring over them, raises them to life the third day.

"For Judah's Lion bursts His chains,
  Crushing the serpent's head ;
And cries aloud through death's domain,
  To wake the imprison'd dead."

There was a very celebrated Easter Sequence, of unknown date and authorship, but certainly earlier than A.D. 1000, called the *Victimæ Paschali.* It is short, picturesque, and simple, and soon came into use for Easter services, and also, being very dramatic in style, formed a striking feature in many Easter Mystery Plays. There was a curious old custom at matins on Easter Day, at which this hymn was much used, connected with the *Easter Sepulchre.* This was a representation of the tomb of our Blessed Lord, sometimes carved in stone, as found in many old churches in England, and sometimes a temporary structure of wood.

On the evening of Maundy Thursday, the Crucifix and Host were taken from the Altar, and placed in the sepulchre ; candles were lighted round, and watchers stood by. In some cases real soldiers kept guard on Easter Eve, to represent the Roman guards, and making the ceremony more impressive. Then, on Easter Sunday, "very early in the morning," the Crucifix and Host were taken out, with every sign of reverence and joy, and placed back on the Altar ; all being done, of course, in memory of Christ's Death, Burial, and Resurrection.   This ceremony is now performed in many churches in Rome.

Here is a description of one of the Easter morning services, at which the *Victimæ Paschali* was sung.   Two boys, vested in white, took their places, one on the right, the other on the left of the High Altar, to represent the angels at the Holy Sepulchre.   Then three deacons, in white dalmatics, representing the three Maries, came from the right side, and stood before the Altar.   The angels ask the three Maries, "Whom seek ye in the sepulchre ?" and they answer, "Jesus of Nazareth." Then the angels, taking off the white altar-cloth, representing the grave-clothes, reply, "He is not here."   The Maries, turning to the choir, sing, "Alleluia, the Lord has risen."   Then, passing down towards the choir, the first Mary sings (first stanza)—

> " Unto the Paschal Victim bring,
>   Christians, your thankful offering."

The second sings (the next stanza of the *Victimæ Paschali*)—

> " The Lamb the sheep hath ransomed,
>   Christ the undefiled,
>   Hath sinners to His God and Father reconciled."

And the third sings (stanza three)—

> " Death and life, in wondrous strife,
>   Came to conflict sharp and sore,
>   Life's Monarch, He that died,   .
>   Now dies no more."

Then the succentor, coming to the first steps of the Altar, asks the first Mary—

"What thou sawest, Mary, say,
As thou wentest on thy way?"

and she answers—

"I saw the slain One's earthly prison,
I saw the glory of the Risen."

The second Mary—

"The witness angels by the cave,
And the garments of the grave."

The third Mary—

"The Lord, my Hope, is risen,
And He before you goes to Galilee."

Then the succentor, pointing to the first Mary and turning to the choir, sings—

"We know that Christ is risen from death indeed,"

and the whole choir join in the last line of the hymn—

"Thou Victor Monarch, for Thy suppliants plead."

Meanwhile, the Maries retire to the vestry, the bishop or succentor begins the Te Deum. This was only one of the many forms of the same service, held after the first lesson, at matins on Easter Day.[1] The translation of the *Victimæ* is that given in the Hymnary and Hymnal Noted, because more literal and true to the dramatic form than the better known translation (A. & M., 131)—

"Christ the Lord is risen to-day."

It is a pity that the third stanza of this is

[1] The hymn is inserted by permission of Messrs. Novello and Co.

omitted, giving the words of the Maries and the angels. A description of a somewhat similar service, in Durham Cathedral, is given by an old writer—

"There was a very solemn service betwixt three and four of the clock in the morning (of Easter Day) in honour of the Resurrection, where two of the eldest monks of the quire came to the Sepulchre, set up upon Good Friday, after the Passion, all covered with red velvet, embroidered with gold, and did then cense it, either of the monks with a pair of silver censers sitting on their knees before the Sepulchre. Then they, both rising, came to the sepulchre, out of which, with great reverence, they took a marvellous beautiful image of our Saviour representing the Resurrection, with a cross in His Hand. Then . . . singing the anthem of *Christus Resurgens*, they brought it to the Altar."

The *Victimæ Paschali* is one of the five sequences kept in the Roman Missal, the others being the *Veni sancte spiritus*, for Pentecost ; the *Dies Iræ*, for funerals ; the *Lauda Sion*, for Corpus Christi ; and the *Stabat Mater*, for festivals of the Blessed Virgin.

VIII.

LATIN HYMNS.

ELEVENTH AND TWELFTH CENTURIES.

" I have no hesitation in saying that I look upon these verses of Bernard as the most lovely, in the same way that the *Dies Iræ* is the most sublime, and the *Stabat Mater* the most pathetic of medieval poems."—DR. NEALE.

WE come now to the eleventh century, and the first name to remember is that of S. *Peter Damiani* (988—1072). He was born at Ravenna, and his early life was very sad. His mother abandoned him as a little baby, but a faithful servant discovered him, and took care of him until the mother relented and took him back. When still very young both parents died, and a brother took compassion on him and had him educated. He became a Benedictine monk, and afterwards rose to be a Cardinal and coadjutor-Pope to Gregory VII. Late in life he retired to the monastery of Santa Croce d'Avellano, and spent the rest of his life in meditation, and in composing sacred verse. He wrote a hymn for Advent, on *Death*, which has been called "the *Dies Iræ* of the individual life." It is translated in the Hymnary—

> " Day of death, in silence speeding,
> On the wings of darkness near,
> How my inmost nature trembles,
> Melting with excess of fear,
> When in sleepless thoughts reclined,
> I depict it to my mind."

One of his most beautiful hymns was the *Ad perennis vitæ fontem*, of which there is a good translation in the Sarum Hymnal—

" For the fount of life eternal thirstily the spirit yearns,
Swift the soul to break her prison in the flesh a prisoner burns,
And like exile, panting, writhing, struggling, homeward ever turns.

Sun, nor moon, nor starry courses, changing seasons, these obey,
For the Lamb is that blest city's light of undeclining ray ;
He, o'er night and time triumphant, bringeth in perpetual day." etc.

A great religious movement, namely, the Crusades, was going on in the twelfth century. Everywhere, throughout Christendom, men's hearts were fired with love and devotion to that Master in Whose honour they bore the Red Cross, and Whose tomb they went to rescue from heathen spoilers. Now, whenever the world has been stirred by great religious revivals or events, great hymns seem to have been written. Just as the Reformation in Germany, and the religious revival of the eighteenth century in England, heralded an outburst of sacred song, the Crusades wrought a religious enthusiasm, expressed in many beautiful hymns. Indeed, the twelfth century has been called the "golden era of the harvest-field of hymnology." The hymns themselves speak of the time in which they were written—of the glories of the *New* Jerusalem, of peace after war, of rest after battle.

The five great hymn-writers of the twelfth century were the two S. Bernards, Adam of S. Victor, Archbishop Hildebert, and Peter the Venerable.

About the year 1140 two monks of the same name, dwelling not more than one hundred and fifty miles from each other, were each composing hymns which were to last, not only for years, but for centuries.

S. Bernard of Clairvaux (1091—1153) was born, of noble parents, in Burgundy. He was among the number of great and famous men who had good *mothers*. Her name was the Lady Aletta; she brought up her children well, and lived a most holy life, and they all became remarkable men and women. Her death-bed made a great impression upon the young Bernard, and at the age of twenty-two he became a monk in the monastery of Citeaux.

This became so crowded that it was thought fit to found another one, so two years after S. Bernard had become an inmate the Abbot chose out twelve monks, representing the Twelve Apostles, with Bernard as their leader, representing our Lord, and going before them, cross in hand. The gates of the convent closed behind them, and they went out into the world, trusting God to show them their future home. They settled in a lonely vale, called "The Valley of Wormwood," and by hard and ceaseless labour they transformed the desolate land into a fertile garden, and the name of the place was changed, and it was called *Clairvaux*—" the Bright Valley." S. Bernard was considered the founder of the order of monks called *Cistercian*, and it is remarkable how many of their houses, like Bolton Abbey in Wharfedale, were built in *valleys*.

S. Bernard had very delicate health, yet he gave himself much manual labour, reaping, digging, and meditating as he worked. He says—" Take the testimony of my own experience, and believe me thou wilt find more in woods than in books, and trees and stones will teach thee more than thou canst learn from man." His life was a very busy one, for he took part in public affairs, and preached in France and Germany, trying to persuade the people to join the second Crusade, and rousing much enthusiasm. But the Crusade proved disastrous, and Bernard was partly blamed for it; and weary of the world and its disappointments, he retired into solitude, to meditate on the love of Christ, and at this time, probably, wrote his famous hymns. The *Jesu dulcis memoria* was a long hymn of forty-eight stanzas, called the *Jubilee Rhythm of the Name of Jesus.* The translations, which form separate hymns, are these—

> " Jesu, the very thought is sweet."
> (Ch. Hy., 402 ; A. & M., 177.)
> " Jesu, the very thought of Thee."
> (A. & M., 178 ; 3 parts.)
> " Jesu, Thy mercies are untold."
> (A. & M., 189.)
> " Jesu, Thou joy of loving hearts."
> (Ch. Hy., 403 ; A. & M., 190.)

And no doubt many other hymns of this nature are translated or adapted from the *Jesu dulcis.* S. Bernard's other famous hymn was the *Salve mundi salutare*, a poem of three hundred and seventy lines, addressed to the different members of the Body of Christ hanging upon the Cross. Tradition says that he wrote it when gazing on a crucifix, when the Figure of Christ appeared to come down from the Cross and embrace him. The German poet, Gerhardt, made a very beautiful translation of this into his own language, and from it is taken our hymn—

> " O sacred Head, surrounded
> By crown of piercing thorn." (A. & M., 111.)

But we must pass on to the second S. Bernard, author of the beautiful *Rhythm of the Heavenly Country*, which has given us our very favourite hymns—

> " Brief life is here our portion."
> (Ch. Hy., 341 ; A. & M., 225.)
> " The world is very evil." (A. & M., 226.)
> " For thee, O dear, dear country."
> (Ch. Hy., 365 ; A. & M., 227.)

"Jerusalem the golden."
(Ch. Hy., 395 ; A. & M., 228.)

S. Bernard of *Cluny* wrote a long poem of three thousand lines, called *De Contemptu mundi ;* and he began his treatise on "the contempt of the world" by a lovely set of verses on the joys and glories of heaven. This was translated by Dr. Neale, and from this translation our hymns are taken. He tells us that it is impossible to give any idea of the beauty of the original Latin verse ; in fact, S. Bernard himself says he believes only the inspiration of the Spirit of God could have enabled him to write it. Many tired wayfarers, many sufferers, worn with pain and trouble, have been soothed and cheered by these beautiful descriptions of the heavenly country. One little child, who was suffering such agonies as the doctors declared to be almost unparalleled, would lie perfectly still while the whole four hundred lines were being read to him.

S. Bernard was born, of English parents, at Morlaix, on the sea-coast of Brittany. He is sometimes called Bernard of *Morlaix*, from his birthplace ; but more often Bernard of *Cluny*, from the celebrated abbey where he became monk under the still more celebrated abbot, Peter the Venerable, himself a hymn-writer. His hymns, however, and those of Hildebert, Archbishop of Tours, are not so famous as those of the two S. Bernards, although many of them are very beautiful. Both were great men in their day, and we hear that Hildebert wrote more than ten thousand verses.

But the *greatest* hymn-writer of the century was Adam of S. Victor, born in Britannia, which may mean Britain, or Brittany. He took his name from the great school of the Abbey of S. Victor, in Paris, where he studied, and where he died, about the year 1192. His hymns show us his deep knowledge of Scripture and of theology, and his fondness for *types*. For instance, in a hymn on Holy Communion, many Old Testament types are given—

> " Honey in the lion's mouth,   .
> Emblem mystical, divine,
> How the sweet and strong combine,
> Cloven rock of Israel's drouth,
> Treasure-house of golden grain,
> By our Joseph laid in store." etc.

Adam wrote a large number of sequences, among which was one for S. Stephen's Day, translated in a most spirited way by Dr. Neale—

> " Yesterday, with exultation." (A. & M., 64.)

Another was for S. John the Evangelist's Day, from which it is possible that Keble may have taken some ideas for his hymn of S. John's Day (A. & M., 67)—

> " Word supreme, before creation."

Two other hymns in A. & M., for Festivals of Apostles and Evangelists (Nos., 620 & 621)—

> " In royal robes of splendour,"

> " Come sing, ye choirs exultant,"

are taken from Adam of S. Victor ; and the hymn by Robert Campbell (A. & M., 434)—

> " Come, pure hearts, in sweetest measures,"

is no doubt adapted from his sequence for the four Evangelists, *Jucundare, plebs fidelis.* Adam also wrote two beautiful Easter sequences, and one for the Invention of the Cross, considered to be his masterpiece—

> " Be the Cross our theme and story,
> We, who in the Cross's glory
> Shall exult for evermore.
> By the Cross the warrior rises,
> By the Cross the foe despises,
> Till he gains the heavenly shore." etc.

The hymn,

" O what the joy and the glory must be " (A. & M., 235),

was written by Abelard (1079—1142), and is in a hymn-book which he wrote for Helöise and the nuns of the Abbey of the Paraclete, and which has been only recently discovered.

To the twelfth, or perhaps the beginning of the thirteenth, century we can trace one of our Advent and three of our Easter hymns, though their authors are unknown—

> "O come, O come, Emmanuel." (A. & M., 49.)
> " The strife is o'er, the battle done."
> (Ch. Hy., 139 ; A. & M., 135.)
> "O sons and daughters, let us sing." (A. & M., 130.)
> "Jesu, the world's redeeming Lord." (A. & M., 141.)

We will finish this chapter by some verses from a *Song of Pilgrims*, translated by Dr. Neale from an MS. of the eleventh century, and probably written at the beginning of the Crusades for the pilgrims to chant as they went on their way—

> " O Christ, our King, give ear !
> O Lord and Maker, hear !
> And guide our footsteps lest they stray.
>
> O ever Three in One,
> Protect our course begun,
> And lead us on our holy way !

E

Thy faithful guardian send,
Thy Angel, who may tend,
And bring us to Thy holy seat.

Defend our onward path,
Protect from hostile wrath,
And to our land return our feet.

And, O good Lord, at last,
Our many wanderings past,
Give us to see Thy realm of light." etc.

IX.

LATIN HYMNS.

THIRTEENTH AND FOLLOWING CENTURIES.

" Nor did they march in silence, but chanted, as they went,
 hymns of hope and joy."—S. CHRYSOSTOM.

IT is rather a curious fact, and worthy of note, that, while all the great hymn-writers of the twelfth century were *French*, those of the thirteenth were *Italian*. All, however, wrote in Latin, except S. Francis of Assisi, whose hymns were in his native language, and therefore come under the heading of Italian hymns.[1] Three of his disciples, Bonaventura, Jacobus de Benedictus, and Thomas of Celano were great hymn-writers.

S. Bonaventura was born in Tuscany, in the year 1221. In his childhood he had a dangerous illness, and his mother, in her grief, brought the little fellow to the good S. Francis, beseeching him to pray for the child's life, and to heal him, and it is said that when S. Francis saw him, he exclaimed, " O buona

[1] See p. 125.

ventura "("O happy chance"); and the mother, in her delight at the boy's recovery, dedicated him to God under that name. He became a friar of the Order of S. Francis, and was distinguished for his great learning. When asked the source of it, he used to point in silence to his Crucifix, meaning that he looked to Christ to guide him in all he undertook. Among other hymns, he wrote one for the hour of the Passion, which has been translated by Mrs. Charles, and is in the Rev. Godfrey Thring's hymn-book. The hymn,

"In the Lord's atoning grief" (A. & M., 105),

is also taken from it.

One of the greatest medieval hymns was the *Stabat Mater*, written, it was said, by Jacobus or Jacopone de Benedictis,[1] who was born at Lodi, in Umbria, of noble parents. He was a lawyer, and full of humour and satire, and lived a secular life until the death of his wife, who was killed by an accident in a theatre. She was a very good woman, and her death made a great impression on him, and he withdrew from the world to join the Order of S. Francis, turning his gifts of poetry to the honour of God. The epitaph on his tombstone at Lodi is a very curious one—" The bones of Jacobus of Lodi, who, a fool for Christ's sake, deluded the world by this strange wile, and seized heaven." The hymn called *Stabat Mater* is founded on S. John xix. 25, S. Luke ii. 35, Zech. xiii. 6, 2 Cor. iv. 10, Gal. vi. 17 ; and consists of ten stanzas of six lines each. It was called " A sequence or prose on the seven griefs of the Blessed Virgin Mary," and was appointed, in

[1] There is no real evidence as to the author.

the Romish Church, to be sung between the Epistle
and Gospel, at High Mass, on the Friday in Passion
Week and on the third Sunday in September. In
the fourteenth century, the Flagellants brought it
into more common use by singing it from town to
town. The words inspired many great composers
to set them to music, amongst others Palestrina,
Pergolesi, Haydn, Rossini, and Dvorak. We keep
part of the *Stabat Mater* in our beautiful Passion
hymn—

"At the Cross her station keeping." (A. & M., 117.)

The twelfth century produced two S. Bernards,
and the thirteenth two S. Thomases, living near to
each other, and writing hymns.

S. Thomas of *Celano*, near Naples, was one of
the eleven disciples of S. Francis d'Assisi, who
first joined him in 1208. These brothers, the
nucleus of the Franciscan Order, were called *Fratres
Minores*, or *lesser brothers*, to remind them that
humility was to be their great virtue. S. Thomas
must have been a great poet, if, as we suppose, he
wrote the famous *Dies Iræ*, "the great medieval
masterpiece of sacred song," and the only example,
in Old Church poetry, of *triple rhyme*. The hymn
has been translated into all the languages of civilized
countries. One of the earliest English renderings
is by Sylvester (1621), a hymn-writer of the reign of
James I. Thirty years later, in the time of Charles
I., another translation was made by Crashaw; and,
in the reign of Charles II., one by the Earl of Ros-
common. His last words were two lines from his
own version of the *Dies Iræ*, uttered with loud
voice—

"My God, my Father, and my Friend,
Do not forsake me at my end."

Then Sir Walter Scott brought his translation into
The Lay of the Last Minstrel—

"That day of wrath, that dreadful day." (A. & M., 206.)

It is found in many hymn-books, and Sir Walter
himself often repeated it on his death-bed. But the
finest and best translation is that by Dr. Irons—

"Day of wrath, O day of mourning,
See fulfilled the prophets' warning,
Heaven and earth in ashes burning."
(Ch. Hy., 355 ; A. & M., 398),

in which the triple rhyme is kept.

This hymn was published in the year 1848, during
the great French Revolution, and it is very interesting to learn how it came to be written. One of the
most dreadful scenes of terror and bloodshed in
Paris during that fearful time was the death of
Monseigneur Affre, the Archbishop of Paris, who
was shot on the 25th of June on the barricade of the
Place de la Bastille, while trying to persuade the
insurgents to cease firing. He was quietly buried
ten days later, and as soon as it was safe, his funeral
sermon was preached in Notre Dame, with a most
solemn and impressive requiem service, and the
Dies Iræ was sung by an immense body of priests.

Dr. Irons was in Paris, and was present at the
service, and he was so much struck with the
solemnity of it all, partly owing to the terror of
the times and to the magnificent way in which the
Dies Iræ was sung, that, as soon as he got away
from the cathedral, he at once composed his translation of the grand old hymn. Dr. Irons was the

son of a Dissenting minister, but became a prebendary of S. Paul's.

The ritual use of the *Dies Iræ* was as a sequence
for the Burial of the Dead, but we often use it as an
Advent hymn.   It is a marvellous description of
the terror of the last day ; yet the hymn is full of
rest and trust in God.   Like the *Stabat Mater*, it
has been set to music by many great composers.
The poet Goethe has woven it in with great effect
to his play of *Faust.*

But we must leave this famous hymn, and hasten
on to the second S. Thomas, called *Aquinas*, son of
a count of Aquino, near Naples, and born in 1227.
He became a friar, not of the Order of S. Francis,
but of S. Dominic.   It is said that his parents were
very anxious to prevent him from taking monastic
vows, and that when he was seventeen he escaped
to a convent at Naples in order to make them,
his mother rushing after him to try and stop it.
Then he took flight, and was waylaid by his two
brothers, who tore his robe from his back and took
him back to the castle.   There he was shut up, and
no one allowed to see him except his two sisters,
whom he converted.   They helped him to escape
again, and let him down in a basket from a window
of the castle, and at last he was allowed to remain
peaceably in his convent.   He was called "the
angelic Doctor," because of his very sweet temper ;
and in spite of his great learning, was so humble
that he received the nickname of " The Ox."   His
daily prayer was—" Give me, O Lord, a noble heart,
which no earthly affection can drag down."   The
famous hymns of S. Thomas Aquinas were written
for the Festival of Corpus Christi, which he induced

Pope Urban IV. to institute in 1264. They are the *Pange lingua gloriosi*—

" Now my soul the mystery telling." (A. & M., 309.)

Adoro te devote, beautifully translated by Dr. Woodford—

" Thee we adore, O hidden Saviour, Thee.
(Ch. Hy., 216 ; A. & M., 312.)

Verbum supernum—

" The heavenly Word proceeding forth." (A. & M., 311.)

The last stanza of this, " O salutaris " (" O saving Victim "), is used in the Romish Church at the Office of Benedictus, and also, sometimes, at High Mass, after the hymn Benedictus. Gounod's beautiful music to it is well known, and sung in many English churches.

The *Lauda Sion*, the great sequence of S. Thomas, was also written for the same festival. It has been found difficult to translate for use in the English Church, because of the doctrine which it teaches, but one canto, the *Ecce panis*, was often used as a separate hymn, and we have it as—

" Lo, the angels' food is given." (A. & M., 310.)

The *O esca viatorum*, another beautiful hymn on Holy Communion, has been said to be by S. Thomas, but is really of later date—

" O Food that weary pilgrims love." (A. & M., 314.)

There was still a *third* S. Thomas, a hymn-writer well known by his famous book, *The Imitation of Christ*. He was called *à Kempis*, from his birthplace *Kempen*, near Düsseldorf. He was born about the year 1380, a century after the two Italian

saints, and died in 1471. He lived a most holy life,
and it is said that when he prayed his face shone
like heaven. His sacred poems were all in Latin,
and are not well known to us, though some have
been translated. One is on " the joys of heaven."
A very favourite hymn, the *Jerusalem luminosa*,
" On the glory of the heavenly Jerusalem, concern-
ing the endowment of the glorified body," has been
ascribed, without good authority, to S. Thomas à
Kempis. It is translated—

> " Light's abode, celestial Salem. (A. & M., 232.)

There is a sequence for the dying in time of
pestilence, which occurs in a Mass arranged by Pope
Clement VI. at Avignon, during a dreadful pestilence, brought over by merchants from the Levant.
All those who heard the Mass were to bear in the
hand a lighted candle, and hold it kneeling, and so
sudden death would not hurt them. It is translated
in the Hymnary—

> " Holy Trinity, before Thee,
>   Lo ! Thy people prostrate fall ;
> Father, Son, and Holy Spirit,
>   Lord, have mercy now on all ;
> Helper of the poor and helpless,
>   On Thy Name Thy servants call.
>
> For our hearts are torn with anguish,
>   All around are fear and woe ;
> And the stoutest hearts are failing,
>   At the dread insidious foe,
> Spreading far and near contagion,
>   Lays the best and fairest low." etc.

Another well-known hymn of the fourteenth
century, of unknown authorship, for Holy Communion, is the prayer, *Anima Christi sanctifia me.*

There are many prose and metrical translations of it—

"Soul of Christ, my soul make pure." etc.

Although all the later medieval hymn-writers seem to have been monks, and to have written their hymns in the cloister, there are many Latin hymns of the fourteenth and fifteenth centuries of *unknown* authorship, and these are some of the best known by their translations—

"Alleluia, song of sweetness." (Ch. Hy., 102 ; A. & M., 82.)

"O come, all ye faithful." (*Adeste fideles.*)
(Ch. Hy., 85 ; A. & M., 59.)

" To the Name of our salvation."
(Ch. Hy., 536 ; A. & M , 179.)

"O love, how deep, how broad, how high." (A. & M., 173)

" Blessed feasts of blessed Martyrs." (A. & M., 440.)

" Who the multitudes can number." (A. & M., 619.)

" Again the Lord's own day is here." (A. & M., 35.)

"With hearts renewed." (A. & M., 159.)

"Zion's daughter, weep no more." (A. & M., 100.)

X.

EARLY ENGLISH HYMNS.

" Give me the making of the people's hymns, and I care not who makes their creeds."

THERE is no doubt that Christian hymns were in use in Britain before Augustine and his monks landed in Kent and brought with them the Latin hymns of Gregory and Ambrose, in the year A.D.

597.   Indeed, the first hymn-writer of whom we
have any record, in the British Isles, was *S. Patrick*,
the second bishop and patron-saint of Ireland.
He was born in 372, most probably near Dumbarton
in Scotland, and at the age of sixteen was carried
off as a slave to Ireland.   There he stayed six
years, feeding swine, and his misfortunes led him
to become a Christian.   He escaped at last, and
went back to his parents, but later in life he
determined to become a missionary to the heathen
Irish; and the legend of his teaching the people
the doctrine of the Holy Trinity by means of a
shamrock leaf is well known.

S. Patrick's Irish hymn is a very famous one.
Tradition says that it was composed after a miracle
in the plains of Tara, where, at a heathen festival
on Easter Sunday, the saint, raising his staff, called
on the Name of Jesus, and the great idol which stood
there fell, broken to pieces, and the king and his
people were converted and baptized.   Then, in his
joy, S. Patrick composed a beautiful hymn, which
was the means of spreading the faith far and near.
It is called *The Breastplate*[1] *of S. Patrick*, and in
the seventh century was ordered to be sung in all
monasteries and churches throughout the whole of
Ireland.   Mrs. Alexander wrote a fine version of
the hymn sung throughout Ireland on S. Patrick's
Day, 1889, and at the enthronement of the Archbishop of York, on the same day, in 1891—

> "I bind unto myself to-day,
> The strong Name of the Trinity,
> By invocation of the same,
> The Three in One and One in Three.

---

[1] Lorica.

I bind unto myself to-day,
   The power of God to hold and lead,
His eye to watch, His might to stay,
   His ear to hearken to my need,
The wisdom of my God to teach,
   His hand to guide, His shield to ward,
The Word of God to give me speech,
   His heavenly host to be my guard.

Christ be with me, Christ within me,
Christ behind me, Christ before me,
Christ beside me, Christ to win me,
Christ beneath me, Christ above me,
Christ in quiet, Christ in danger,
Christ in hearts of all that love me,
Christ in mouth of friend or stranger." etc.

A hymn was written in honour of S. Patrick by Sechnall, his nephew, about the year 458, which was said to be a coat of mail to all who repeated it; and other hymns of the ancient Irish Church have been found. Music was largely used in worship in this branch of the Christian Church, and was very probably in the Eastern style, for the Celtic Church is said to be of Eastern origin. We read of a hymn which was sung after the prayer of consecration, during the communion of the clergy and before that of the people. This was the

   "Sancti venite,
   Corpus Christi sumite,"

which Dr. Neale has translated so beautifully—

"Draw nigh and take the Body of the Lord,
And drink the holy Blood for you outpoured."
              (Ch. Hy., 207 ; A. & M. 313.)

One of the old legends relates how a choir of angels was heard in the Church of S. Sechnall, in Ireland, chanting this hymn.

Crossing over to the west coast of Scotland, we find that S. Columba, the missionary, in his lonely island of Iona, besides his translation of the Psalms, wrote a noble hymn called the *Altus Prosator*, containing the substance of the Creeds in one hundred and fifty lines; and it is said that his voice was so powerful that he could be heard chanting a mile off. In Wales, another birthplace of Christianity, we have already heard of the Alleluia battle, and there is little doubt that the Britons were renowned for their fine voices. The historian, Gildas, speaks of "the musical voices of the young, sweetly singing the praises of God."

There is a very old Saxon hymn, *To the Holy Trinity*, from which I believe our Trinity Sunday hymn is taken—

"All hail, adored Trinity" (A. & M., 158);

and in the service of the Anglo-Saxon Church a rendering of the Apostles' Creed used to be sung to the harp, and is given in a book on the early Church, beginning—

"Father of unchanging might,
Set above the welkin's height,
Thro' the unsullied tracts of air,
Didst in their own space prepare,
And the solid earth as fast,
With its deep foundation cast." etc.

Cædmon, the swineherd of Whitby, wrote a wonderful sacred hymn, beginning with the creation of the world, and going on to the Redemption ; and we read of Aldhelm, abbot of Malmesbury, the saintly man who, laying aside all state and dignity for awhile, and sitting on a rustic bridge over the Avon, sang David's psalms to David's strings with

harp in hand. Dr. Porter, in his *Lives of the Saints,*
gives us a description of this :

"In King Elfred's time many of S. Aldhelme's ditties were
sung in England. One thing related of this purpose by
King Elfred is most worthy of memoir. The people of those
times, being yet rude rustics, and verie negligent in the
Divine service, seemed to come to church but for fashion's
sake (as manie now-a-days doe), where they made noe long
stay, but as soon as the misterie of masse was done, they
flocked homewards without any more adoe. Our prudent
Aldhelme, perceiving this small devotion in the people,
placed himself on a bridge over which they were to passe
from church to their villages, where, when the hasty multitude
of people came (whose minds were already on their beef-
pots at home), he began to put forth his voice with all the
musical art he could, and charmed their ears with his songs.
For which, when he grew to be grateful and plausible to
that rustic people, and perceived that his songs flowed into
their eares and mindes, and the great pleasure and content-
ment of both, he beganne by little and little to mingle his
ditties with more serious and holy matters, taken out of the
Holy Scriptures, and by that meanes brought them in time
to a feeling of devotion and to spend their Sunday and holy
daies with farre greater profit to their owne soules."

Another picture, this, of the great power and
value of hymn-singing.

Aldhelm died in the year 709, and about the
time of his death another saint, still more celebrated
and learned, was writing hymns far away in the
extreme north of England, at Jarrow-on-the-Tyne.
This was the *Venerable Bede*, born about A.D.
673, at Wearmouth, and when seven years old
given into the care of Benedict Biscop, to be
brought up to the religious life. He was ordained
deacon at the age of nineteen, and after, priest, and
spent his life in the religious house at Jarrow, becoming the most cultivated man of his age and

country. He wrote at pleasure in prose or verse,
in Anglo-Saxon or in Latin, and on an immense
variety of subjects. He was called the father of
English learning ; but, unlike so many very clever
men, he kept his faith in, and love of God, and
this made him wonderfully humble. This is the
prayer with which he ends the story of his labours
and of the forty-five works he had written—

"O good Jesu, Who hast deigned to refresh my soul with
the sweet stream of knowledge, grant to me that I may one
day mount to Thee, Who art the source of all wisdom, and
remain for ever in Thy Divine Presence."

Among his many writings was "A Book of
Hymns, in several sorts of metre and rhyme." These
were written in Latin, but he also composed them
in Anglo-Saxon. One of them is translated in
A. & M., 415—

"The great forerunner of the morn."

Two others are well known : for the Ascension,
and for the Feast of the Holy Innocents—

"The hymn for conquering martyrs raise
The victor Innocents we praise,
Whom in their woe earth cast away,
But heaven with joy received to-day :
Whose Angels see the Father's face,
World without end, and hymn His grace,
And while they chant unceasing lays,
The hymn for conquering martyrs raise."

The account of Bede's death is most beautiful,
and is told by one of his monks, an eye-witness—

"Nearly a fortnight before Easter he was seized with an
extreme weakness, in consequence of his difficulty of breath-
ing, but without pain. He continued thus until Ascension
Day, always joyous and happy, giving thanks to God day and

night. He gave us our lessons daily, and employed the rest
of his time in chanting psalms, and passed every night, after
a short sleep, in joy and thanksgiving, but without closing
his eyes. From the moment of waking he resumed his
prayers and praises to God, with his arms in the form of a
cross. He also sang anthems. . . . At this time he was
finishing a translation of the Gospel of S. John into our
English tongue, for the use of the Church. On the eve of
the Feast of Ascension, at the first dawn of morning, he
desired that what had been commenced should be quickly
finished. In the evening the young secretary said to him,
' Beloved Master, there remains only one verse which is not
written.' 'Write it then, quickly,' he said. And the young
man cried, 'It is finished.' 'You say truly "It is finished,"'
said he. ' Support my head in thine arms, for I desire to sit
in the holy place where I am accustomed to pray, that sitting
there, I may call upon my Father.' Thus, lying on the floor
of his cell, he sang for the last time, ' Glory be to the Father,
and to the Son, and to the Holy Spirit'; and with these
last words on his lips,—a fitting close to one who had sung
God's praises in his life—he gave up the ghost."

The last early English hymn-writer we shall
mention is King Alfred himself, who, amongst his
other writings, is said to have composed Latin
hymns. A translation of one of them, for the
morning, said, though without proof, to be by him,
is given in the Sarum Hymnal—

"As the sun doth daily rise,
Brightening all the morning skies,
So to Thee, with one accord,
Lift we up our hearts, O Lord.

Day by day provide us food,
For from Thee come all things good ;
Strength unborn our souls afford,
From Thy Living Bread, O Lord.

Be our Guard in sin and strife,
Be the Leader of our life,
Lest like sheep we stray abroad,
Stay our wayward feet, O Lord," etc.

XI.

PSALMS IN VERSE.

" Has David, Christ to come foreshowed ?
Can Christians then aspire,
To mend the harmony that flowed
From his prophetic lyre ?

Let David's pure, unaltered lays
Transmit through ages down
To Thee, O David's Lord, our praise,
To Thee, O David's Son."—SAMUEL WESLEY.

A VERY great number of efforts have been made
in England to versify the Psalter, but with very
little success.   We have heard already of Aldhelm,
the good Saxon abbot, who, harp in hand, taught
the people to sing, on the bridge over the Avon.
It is supposed that he made a metrical version
of most of the Psalms, for a Saxon version was
found in an old French monastery ; the first fifty
in prose, the rest in verse, and the metrical part, at
any rate, is said to be by Aldhelm.   He very wisely
tried to suit the meaning of the Psalms to the
customs of his day, and the homely imagery suited
the people.   For instance, he speaks of the peace-
stool, or stone seat, placed near the altar in English
churches, as a place of refuge, where culprits might
be free for seven days.   " *God is the place of peace*
to the poor " (Ps. xcix.).   " The Lord God is become
my *peace-stool*" (Ps. cxiv. 22).   The harp-songs, as
the metrical versions were called, were not only
simple, but really poetical and devotional.   These
are two examples (from Churton's *Early English
Church*)—

"As the beacon fire by night,
That the host of Israel led,
Such the glory fair and bright
Round the good man's dying bed ;
'Tis a beacon, bright and fair,
Telling that the Lord is there."—Ps. cxvi. 15.

"Lord, to me Thy minsters are
Courts of honour, passing fair,
And my spirit deems it well
There to be and there to dwell,
Heart and flesh would soon be there,
Lord, Thy life, Thy love, to share."
Ps. lxxxiv. 1, 2.

To come to later days, four great attempts, besides many smaller ones, were made to put the Psalms into English verse.

The first was that of Sternhold and Hopkins, in 1551, the time of the Reformation. Thomas Sternhold was groom of the robes to Henry VIII. and Edward VI., and John Hopkins was a clergyman in Suffolk. Fuller says of them that they were "men whose piety was better than their poetry," and his words are very true, as may be seen from the following examples—

"So many buls do compass me,
That be full strong of head,
Yea, buls so fat, as though they had
In Basan field been fed."

"They shall heap sorrow on their heads,
Which run as they were mad ;
To offer to the idol gods,
Alas, it is too bad !"

Yet, in spite of the indifference in their composition, these Psalms of the Old Version became most popular, and great crowds of people used to gather round S. Paul's Cross and sing them, "sadly

F

annoying the mass-priests and the devil," as Bishop
Jewel says.   We still keep in our hymn-book two
psalms from a later edition of the Old Version,
neither of which, however, is by Sternhold or
Hopkins.   The first is the Old Hundredth,

> " All people that on earth do dwell,"

probably written by William Kethe, a native of
Scotland and a refugee with John Huss at Geneva ;
and the second, Psalm cxliii.,

> " O Lord, turn not Thy face from me,
> Who lie in woful state,"

supposed to be by John Marchant (1380).

The public singing of the Psalms ceased under
Queen Mary's reign, though they were used
privately more than ever ; and when Queen Elizabeth came to the throne, nothing could exceed the
enthusiasm of the people at being allowed to sing
them again, when, in June 1559, permission was
given that they should be sung in public worship.

Many smaller attempts at versification were
attempted at this time by Queen Elizabeth herself,
by Fairfax, Lord Bacon, and other poets and theo-
logians.   Spenser versified the seven penitential
psalms, but these, unfortunately, have been lost.
Sir Philip Sydney and his sister, Lady Pembroke,
made, between them, a metrical version of the
Psalms, which, though never used in public worship,
has, perhaps, more poetry in it than any other.
Here is a verse from it—

> " O Lord, in me there lieth nought,
> But to Thy search revealed lies,
> For when I sit,
> Thou makest it,

No less Thou notest when I rise.
Yea, closest closet of my thought,
Hath open windows to Thine eyes."—Ps. cxxxix.

Another version, made in 1612, was Ainsworth's
Book of Psalms, carried by the Pilgrim Fathers to
New England ; and Longfellow speaks of it in his
Courtship of Miles Standish. Priscilla sits spinning
and

" Singing the Hundredth Psalm, the grand old Puritan
anthem,
Music that Luther sang to the sacred words of the
Psalmist,
Full of the breath of the Lord, consoling and comforting
many."

This is the part of the psalm most quaintly
rendered—

" Shout to Jehovah, all the earth,
Serve ye Jehovah with gladness,
Before Him come with singing mirth,
Know that Jehovah He God is.

It's He that made us, and not wee,
His sheep and folk of His feeding ;
O with confession enter yee,
His gates, His courtyards with praising."

There is a still more curious rendering of Psalm
cxxxvii., which no doubt the Pilgrims sang with
heart as well as voice—

" Jehovah's song now sing shall wee,
Within a foreign people's land ;
Jerusalem, if I doo Thee
Forget—forget let my right hand."

This " Book of Psalms, Englished both in prose
and metre," contains tunes, popular melodies ; as
Ainsworth says, " the gravest and the easiest."
The second *great* metrical version was the *Scottish*

Psalter, adopted in the time of the Commonwealth. It was compiled by Francis Rouse, an M.P., and has been used in Scottish kirks from May 1st, 1650, until the present time. A family named Wedder-burn, at Dundee, composed many of the psalms; and John Knox brought some of them from Germany, where he had heard Luther's hymns. They have always been dear to the hearts of the Scotch people, and were sung from many a rocky glen and wild moor by the fugitive Covenanters. An account of the use of one of them, at the battle of Drumclog, is given in *Old Mortality*—

"As the horsemen halted their lines on the ridge of the hill, their trumpets and kettledrums sounded a bold and warlike flourish of menace and defiance, that rang along the waste like the shrill summons of a destroying angel. The wanderers, in answer, united their voices, and sent forth, in solemn modulation, the first two verses of the seventy-sixth Psalm, according to the metrical version of the Scottish Kirk—

> "In Judah's land God is well known,
> His Name in Israel great,
> In Salem is His tabernacle,
> In Zion is His seat.

> There arrows of the bow He brake,
> The shield, the sword, the war.
> More glorious Thou than hills of prey,
> More excellent art far." etc.

This Psalter of Rouse's was added to in 1745, when *Paraphrases of other parts of the Bible* were admitted. These were really hymns, adhering, as closely as possible, to the words of Scripture, and we keep some in our books now. The Ascension hymn (see 2 Cor. v. 1)—

> "Where high the heavenly temple stands"
>   (Ch. Hy., 552 ; A. & M., 201),

by Michael Bruce, the son of a weaver, who died in
1767, at the early age of twenty-one ;

" The people that in darkness sat " (Is. ix. 2), (A. & M., 80,)

by John Morrison ; and

" How bright those glorious spirits shine " (Rev. vii. 14—17),
(Ch. Hy., 384 ; A. & M., 438,)

by William Cameron, are three of the most widely-
known of these paraphrases.

Archbishop Sandys (1577—1643) wrote many
paraphrases of Psalms, and Milton made several
metrical versions. One, the cxxxvi., was written
when he was a school-boy of fifteen. It begins—

" Let us, with a gladsome mind,
Praise the Lord, for He is kind."

The refrain of each verse has been borrowed in our
well-known Harvest hymn—

" For His mercies aye endure,
Ever faithful, ever sure."

In Milton's time there was a great talk about
making a New Version of the Psalms, to super-
sede that of Sternhold and Hopkins ; but though
James I. himself tried his hand at the work, nothing
was really done until 1696, when the *third* great
Psalter, that of the Restoration, by Nahum Tate
and Nicholas Brady, both Irishmen, was published,
and permitted to be used in churches and chapels.
This New Version was almost as dull and dry
as the Old, but a few of the Psalms still live in our
hymn-books.

" Through all the changing scenes of life " (Ps. xxxiv.).
(Ch. Hy., 530 ; A. & M., 290.)

" Have mercy, Lord, on me " (Ps. li.). (A. & M., 249.)

" O God of hosts, the mighty Lord " (Ps. lxxxiv.).
(Ch. Hy., 443 ; A. & M., 237.)
" Ye boundless realms of joy " (Ps. cxlviii.) ; and
" As pants the hart " (Ps. xlii.)
(Ch. Hy., 334 ; A. & M., 238.)

A supplement to the Psalter was added in 1703, containing some hymns, notably Tate's famous Christmas paraphrase—

" While shepherds watched their flocks by night."
(See S. Luke ii. 8—14.)

At later dates were added Bishop Ken's morning and evening hymns, and

" Hark the herald angels sing,"

" High let us swell our tuneful notes,"

" My God, and is Thy table spread,"

" Jesus Christ is risen to-day,"

" Christ from the dead is raised again,"

the only hymns sung in the churches in the days of our grandparents.

The *fourth* and last great Psalter was that of *Watts*, in the early days of the great evangelical revival ; but this was more of a hymn-book based upon the Psalter, and as we may come to his hymns at some future time, we will pass it over now. Two well-known psalms from his book are—

" O God, our help in ages past " (Ps. xc.).
(Ch. Hy., 446 ; A. & M., 165.)

" Jesus shall reign where'er the sun " (Ps. lxxii.).
(Ch. Hy. 407 ; A. & M. 220.)

Later still, Keble wrote what is called the Oxford Psalter, and he, like Sternhold, rendered the Psalms from the original Hebrew.

Three metrical versions by Lyte are popular—

"Far from my heavenly home" (Ps. cxxxvii.).
(Ch. Hy., 358 ; A. & M., 284.)
"Pleasant are Thy courts above" (Ps. lxxxiv.).
(Ch. Hy., 483 ; A. & M., 240.)
"Praise, my soul, the King of heaven" (Ps. ciii.).
(Ch. Hy., 484 ; A. & M., 298.)

Montgomery wrote a good version of Ps. lxii.,

"Hail to the Lord's Anointed"
(Ch. Hy., 379 ; A. & M., 219) ;

and Sir Robert Grant gave us Ps. cviii.—

"O worship the King" (Ch. Hy., 477 ; A. & M., 167.)

The most modern are three good versions by Sir Henry Baker—

"The King of love my Shepherd is." (A. & M., 197.)
"Rejoice to-day with one accord." (A. & M., 378.)
"Praise ! O praise our God and King." (A. & M., 381.)

XII.

CHRISTMAS CAROLS.

" Then came the merry masquers in,
And carols roared with blithesome din.
If unmelodious was the song,
It was a hearty note and strong ;
Who lists, may in their mumming see
Traces of ancient mystery."

THE word *Carol* is taken from the Latin *cantare*, to *sing*, and *rola*, an interjection of joy—or from the Italian *carolare*, "to sing songs of joy." Carols were originally accompanied by a *dance*, and we find that, in the earliest ages of mankind, both song and dance were employed as acts of Divine worship, whether of the true God or of heathen deities. Choral dancing was a great part of Hebrew worship, and instances of its use abound in the Bible. "Let us praise His Name in the dance," etc.

This choral dancing was kept up in Christian times, and we still see it in the rhythmic movements of the chorus at Ober Ammergau. An old proverb of the fourteenth century says :—" The French *sing* or *pipe*, the English *carol*, the Spaniards *wail*, the Germans *howl*, the Italians *caper.*" Carols have survived in England, but the dancing with them has almost entirely disappeared, except in the case of some of the mummers.

The *Gloria in excelsis* was the first Christmas Carol, and many others have since been founded upon the angels' words : yet, strange to say, no carols from the early Christian Church have come down to us. The reason probably is that, in earlier times, Christmas was kept as a quiet, religious season, partly, no doubt, on account of the persecutions, which made the Christians refrain from any outward expressions of joy, at any particular festival. Then, gradually, the heathen rites and customs connected with the New Year were joined to the religious rites, and when the Christians could meet without fear, Christmas became the great time for joyful festivity.

Some of the earliest carols were sung in Italy, in the time of S. Francis of Assisi. There had been a great deal of heresy on the subject of the Incarnation, and S. Francis, who wished to make the ignorant people understand and realize it better, asked leave of the Pope to celebrate Christmas in a new way.

After obtaining permission, he and his monks set forth to a little village called Græcia, near Assisi, and with great pains they prepared in the church a representation of the Nativity. On Christmas Eve the villagers came to the church, carrying lighted torches, and when they saw the strange new scene, the manger filled with hay, the ox and ass standing in their places, the Virgin and her Child, and heard the hymns or carols sung by S. Francis and his friars, we read that "they poured forth praise to God for His wondrous love to man."

Indeed, the effect upon the people was so wonderful, that we are told that S. Francis stood by the manger all night long, sighing for joy, and giving God thanks that by this means the hearts of the people had been touched. This is the first account of a *mystery* in Italy. In England, the mystery, miracle, and morality plays arose much in the same way. The clergy wished to bring home to the people the great facts of Bible history, and the lives and legends of the saints. So, on great festivals, when the time came for the lesson, it was not *read*, but *realized*—acted in the church by the clergy, while the choir sang appropriate hymns and carols. When the crowd became too great, the plays were removed from the inside to the outside of the church, and finally, when the people began to trample on the graves in the churchyards, platforms were erected in unconsecrated ground, and gradually the laity began to take part, and the plays became most popular, until the Reformation put a stop to them. The connection between the original service and the plays was kept up by the carols and hymns of the choristers. This is a description of one of the plays, called *The Massacre of the Innocents.*

First, a procession of children in white robes (to represent the Holy Innocents) marched through the cloisters of the monastery, chanting, " How glorious is Thy kingdom ; send down, O Lord, Thy Lamb." Then the Lamb appeared, represented by a man, carrying a banner, bearing a figure of the Lamb, and taking his place at the head of the children. Meanwhile Herod, seated on his throne, gave his sword to his armour-bearer, and the children still went on singing, " Hail, Lamb of God, O hail ! " Then came the mother, entreating mercy, while the children fell dead. As Rachel appeared, an angel sang, " Suffer the little children to come to Me," and at his voice the children entered the choir, and the Te Deum was sung. Some of these plays have been found in MS., and so we have become possessed of the carols found in them. Many others of the carols called *traditional* would be sung first during the miracle plays, and by the fifteenth century carol-singing was widely spread all over England, and waits and mummers went about singing for money and for food.

Many of the carols which have come down to us from this time contain Latin words ; and some are half-Latin, half-English. This speaks of the days when the Church service was still said in Latin, and when the wish began to have it in " a language understanded of the people." For instance, the carol,

"When Christ was born of Mary free,"

has for its refrain, *In excelsis gloria.* It was found in the Harleian MS. of the year 1500. A still more curious one, dating also from the fifteenth century—

"A Babe is born, all of a maid" (No. 48,[1] S. & S.),

has for the *last* line of each verse the *first* line of some well-known ancient Latin hymn—

> "A Babe is born, all of a maid,
> To bring salvation unto us;
> No more are we to sing afraid,
> *Veni, Creator spiritus.*"

The other Latin hymns ending the verses are—

> "*O lux beata Trinitas.*"
> "*A solis ortus cardine.*" } Hymns by S. Ambrose.
> "*Jam lucis orto sidere.*"
> "*Gloria tibi Domine.*"

Other traditional carols of the fifteenth century, or thereabouts, are given in Stainer's and Bramley's book. One, from the *Towneley Mysteries*—

"The angel and the shepherds" (No. 60);

another, from the *Coventry Mysteries*—

"The Coventry Carol" (No. 61);

and

"The Virgin and Child" (No. 25),

a very beautiful one.

Passing on to the sixteenth century, we find a good many carols and songs in the Elizabethan era. One of the best is by Robert Southwell, a

---

[1] Stainer and Bramley's *Christmas Carols*, published by Novello.

Jesuit priest, who was sent in the year 1584, when only twenty-four, as a missionary to England. There was a very bitter feeling in England at that time against the Roman Catholics, and a few years after his arrival in England, Southwell was arrested and imprisoned in the Tower. There he lingered for three years, and on February 22, 1594, after having suffered ten times the tortures of the rack, he was executed. His carol begins thus—

> " Behold a silly [1] tender Babe,
>   In freezing winter night,
> In homely manger trembling lies,
>   Alas ! a piteous sight :
> The inns are full, no man will yield
>   This little Pilgrim bed ;
> But forced He is with silly beasts
>   In crib to shroud His head." (No. 47.)

Ben Jonson is the author of the carol—

> " I sing the Birth was born to-night " (No. 55).

The well-known carols—

> " God rest you, merry gentlemen " (No. 1),

and

> " I saw three ships come sailing in " (No. 64),

also belong, probably, to the sixteenth century.

During the Commonwealth the singing of carols was more or less subdued, but at the Restoration they broke out again.

Herrick, the poet, has left us quite a picture of the Christmas season of his time in his poems. He wrote a carol which was sung before the king at Whitehall.

---

[1] Simple.

" What sweeter music can we bring,
Than a carol for to sing,
The Birth of this our heavenly King.
Awake the voice ! awake the string,
Heart, ear, and eye, and everything.

. . . .

The Darling of the world is come,
And fit it is we find a room,
To welcome Him.
     The nobler part
Of all the house here is the heart ;
Which we will give Him, and bequeath
This holly and this ivy wreath ;
To do Him honour, Who's our King,
And Lord of all this revelling."

This is only part of the carol, which was sung, apparently, by two choruses, or by a single voice and a chorus.

Another Christmas poet, on the side of the Parliament, was George Wither, who wrote many quaint and beautiful verses. His carol begins—

" As on the night before this happy morn,
A blessed angel unto shepherds told,
Where (in a stable) He was poorly born,
Whom nor the earth, nor heaven of heavens can hold."

William Austin (1630) wrote three carols for Christmas, one of which is well known—

" All this night bright angels sing." (No. 41.)

The eighteenth century brought us very few carols, but during the nineteenth there has been a great revival of them. Coleridge wrote his—

" The shepherds went their hasty way,
And found the lowly stable shed" (No. 63),

in 1799, just at the dawn of the century ; and many modern carols, written since then, are very

good.   Dr. Neale has given us two very popular
ones, imitations of old carols—

"Good Christian men, rejoice,"
and
"Good King Wenceslas looked forth."

Other modern carols are too numerous to mention.   Carols were, and are still, popular in other
countries besides England; in fact, Germany
possesses even more than we do.   One of the most
celebrated is Luther's carol, written for his little
son Hans—

"From highest heaven I come to tell
The gladdest news that ere befell;
These tidings true to you I bring,
And of them I will say and sing.

To you this day is born a Child,
Of Mary, chosen Virgin, mild;
That blessed Child, so sweet and kind,
Shall give you joy and peace of mind." etc.

A very sad story is told in connection with this.
It used to be sung by a boy who was let down
from the roof of a church, dressed as an angel;
but one day, sad to relate, the rope broke, and the
boy was killed, and this put an end to a very
beautiful but dangerous Christmas custom.

There are Spanish and Besançon carols in Stainer
and Bramley's book (Nos. 36 and 49).   Indeed, in
whatever country Christmas is kept at all, it is
kept with *singing*.

XIII.

GERMAN HYMNS.

"There is a certain country called Germany, wherein dwell
Christians, and of a truth very pious ones ; who, as you
know, often come as pilgrims into our land, with their
long staves and great boots ; and amid the most sultry
heat, and bathed in sweat, yet visit all the thresholds of
the holy shrines, and sing hymns of praise to God and all
His saints."—*S. Francis of Assisi to his Monks*, 1221.

No other country is so rich in hymns as Germany ;
and we shall find that some of our favourite hymns
are translated from the German. The grandest
of them had their origin in troublous times, in the
storms of the Reformation, or the perils of the
Thirty Years' War ; indeed, it has been said that
"the Church hymn, in the strict sense of the term,
as a *popular religious lyric*, in praise of God, to be
sung by the congregation in public worship, was
born with the German Reformation."

From the earliest times we hear of the love of
the German race for song, and how they sang
hymns in their heathen worship, and pictured
heaven as echoing with the songs of the brave
heroes who had fallen in battle. About the sixth
century, missionaries spread the Christian faith
throughout Germany, and brought in with them
Latin hymns ; but we hear of no hymns written in
Germany until the ninth century. Then it was
that Notker, the monk of S. Gall, wrote his famous
sequence hymn, *Media vita*.[1] This was afterwards translated into German by Luther. These

[1] See p. 52.

Latin sequence hymns gave rise to the earliest
German hymns. The only part that the people
had to take at that time in the Church service was
to utter continually during the service the words,
"*Kyrie leison, Christe elcison.*"[1] Soon after Notker
started the idea by his sequence hymns, the priests
began to write irregular verses which ended with
Kyrie eleison, and from this the early German
hymns were called *Leisen*. At first these were
not used at Mass, but only on pilgrimages and at
festivals. In the time of the Crusades these *Leisen*
became much more common, and at last they were
introduced into the churches, and sung at Mass.
One for Easter became the first verse of one of
Luther's hymns—

> " Christ the Lord is risen
> Out of Death's dark prison,
> Let us all rejoice to-day,
> Christ shall be our hope and stay.
> Kyrie eleison,
> Alleluia, Alleluia, Alleluia."

Special songs, too, were written for the Crusades,
to be sung on pilgrimages, such as—

> " Kyrie eleison, Christe eleison—
> O help us now, Thou Holy Ghost,
> O Thou most Blessed Voice of God,
> To tread with joy the toilsome road
> Toward thee, Jerusalem.
> Kyrie eleison."

Many Latin hymns, too, were translated into
German at this time, and used in cathedrals and
churches. Mystery and miracle plays came into

---

[1] " Lord, have mercy upon us. Christ, have mercy upon
us."

fashion, and hymns and carols were written for them. In the fifteenth century Henry of Laufen-burg, a priest of Freiburg, translated many Latin hymns, and wrote some of mixed Latin and German. There is a lovely little cradle-song of his, which has been well translated by Miss Wink-worth and made into a baptismal hymn (Ch. Hy., 223)—

"Lord Jesus Christ, our Lord most dear,
As Thou wast once an Infant here,
So give this child of Thine, we pray,
Thy grace and blessing day by day.
O Holy Jesu, Lord Divine,
We pray Thee, guard this child of Thine."

But it was not until Luther's time that hymn-singing during Church service became general in Germany. We are told that "it was on the wings of hymns that the Reformation flew through Ger-many." Wandering minstrels had been popular for some time ; and now, instead of the songs of love and war written by the minnesingers, they got hold of the last new hymn of Luther, or of some kindred spirit, and sang it in the streets. A Jesuit remarked, " The songs of Luther have killed more souls than his books and his words."

Luther was born November 10, 1485, at Eisleben, a little village in Germany. He was always very fond of music and poetry, and his after-dinner recreation was playing on the lute, and singing with his children or his friends. Once, we are told, he was sitting at his window, when he heard a blind beggar sing. " Ah," he thought, " if only I could make Gospel songs which people would sing, and which would spread themselves up and down the cities!" The wish was father to the

G

thought, and after his imprisonment in the Wart-
burg, in 1522, he began to try and alter the service
of the Church, to introduce hymns, and to compose
them himself, and translate them from the Latin.
He says—" It is my intention, after the example
of the prophets and the ancient Fathers, to make
German psalms for the people; that is, spiritual
songs, whereby the Word of God may be kept
alive among them by singing."

Luther has been called "The *Ambrose* of German hymnology"; for his hymns, like those of
S. Ambrose, are simple and strong, full of Church
doctrine, and express great thoughts in very clear
language. Next to the Bible in German, his hymns
proved the best means of spreading the reformed
doctrines. Eight of Luther's hymns were psalms
in verse, the best known being Ps. xlvi.—" Ein
Feste Burg," the Marseillaise of the Reformation,
as it has been called, and the national hymn of
Germany. He is said to have composed it on the
road to Wurms, in the year 1521. It has always
been a favourite hymn in Germany, and Luther
himself composed the Chorale, which Mendelssohn
has woven into the *Reformation Symphony*. The
hymn and tune were sung over Luther's grave, at
Wittenberg, in February 1546, and the first line is
cut on his tombstone—

"A sure stronghold our God is He,
A trusty shield and weapon."[1]

Another of Luther's famous psalm-hymns was
Ps. cxxx.—

"Out of the depths I cry to Thee,
Lord God! Oh, hear my prayer."[2]

---

[1] *Lyra Germanica*, 235.   [2] *Ibid.*, 282.

This was composed in 1524, in the midst of his troubles, was also sung over his grave, and has ever since been one of the funeral hymns of Germany.

The hymn—

> "Great God, what do I see and hear?"
> (Ch. Hy., 375 ; A. & M., 52),

has wrongly been called "Luther's hymn." It was written, in 1586, by Ringwaldt, a village pastor, who took the idea of it from the *Dies Iræ*. He lived in a time of famine, pestilence, and trouble. The tune, however, is almost certainly by Luther.

All Luther's hymns were thoroughly congregational, and intended, not for private use, but for public worship ; they show his deep faith and devotion, his trust and courage, though they are plain and rugged, like the man himself. As soon as they were printed, pedlars carried them about the country for sale, and none of the arts of the Roman priests could stop their circulation. They filled a gap, and met with hearty response wherever they went. Some were written for children, and the Te Deum, Ten Commandments, Lord's Prayer, and Nunc Dimittis were put into verse.

Luther had two friends who were hymn-writers like himself—Justus Jonas and Paul Eber. Jonas was a clever young lawyer, who helped Luther in translating the Psalms into German verse. Eber was the son of a tailor, and as he was passionately fond of books, his father sent him to college at Nuremburg. He was much persecuted on account of his faith, and being very sensitive, his health gave way. His hymns are very touching, and full of pathos. Two for the dying are very popular in Germany.

We must speak next about the hymns of the Bohemian Brethren. Christianity was introduced into Bohemia by two Greek monks in the eighth century, and three centuries later, this ancient Church of Bohemia separated itself from the Roman Church, and tried to keep the native language in public worship, as the Waldenses did in Italy. But the Brethren were persecuted by the Popes, and after many sufferings, they had a district assigned to them in the borders of Silesia and Moravia, where they continued their old form of worship under the name of the United Brethren. The persecution continued until the Reformation allowed them to worship in peace.

The Bohemian race are very musical, and they used many hymns in public worship. Michael Weiss, one of their leaders, who lived in Luther's time, published the hymns of the Brethren, translated into German. One is the well-known Easter hymn—

> "Christ the Lord is risen again."
> (Ch. Hy., 133 ; A. & M., 136.)

Another is a most beautiful evening hymn—

> "Now God be with us, for the night is closing,
> The light and darkness are of His disposing,
> And 'neath His Shadow here to rest we yield us,
>   For He will shield us.
> Let evil thoughts and spirits flee before us,
> Till morning cometh, watch, O Master, o'er us,
> In soul and body Thou from harm defend us,
>   Thine angels send us."

A good old man, named Nicolas Herrmann, precentor of Joachimstal, wrote two beautiful

hymns (1560) ; one, a translation from the Latin,
sung at many German funerals—

> " Now hush your cries, and shed no tear,
> On such death none should look with fear,
> He died a faithful Christian man,
> And with his death true life began.
>
> The buried grain of wheat must die,
> Withered and worthless long must lie,
> Yet springs to light all sweet and fair,
> And proper fruits shall richly bear." etc.[1]

Nicolas loved music passionately, and pictured
heaven as a place where " every organist will take
some holy text and strike upon his organ and lute,
and every one will be able to sing at sight, by
himself, four or five different parts, and there will
be no confusion or mistake."

The last hymn-poet we shall name is Hans
Sachs, the last of the master-singers and first of the
new style of modern poets, who lived at Nuremburg, and was born there in 1494, during a dreadful
plague, and became a shoemaker-poet.

XIV.

GERMAN HYMNS.

THE THIRTY YEARS' WAR.

" Whenever the Holy Ghost inspireth a new hymn, it is His
wont to inspire some one with a good tune to fit it."

THOSE are the words of a very old writer, but
even in our own time we have proof that really

[1] *Lyra Germanica*, 632.

inspired words bring with them really inspired tunes.

This was the case, certainly, with two hymns, written at the end of the sixteenth century, by Nicolai, a pastor in Westphalia. He wrote for them such fine, stirring tunes, that they have been called the king and queen of chorales. During the year 1597 a dreadful pestilence was raging in the little town of which he was pastor, and in a very short time more than 1400 people died. From his window Nicolai could see the funerals passing to the church, and he began to meditate a great deal on eternal life, and to study *The City of God*, by S. Augustine. Two years later he published a book on Life Eternal, to which he added the two hymns which became so popular all over Germany. Those who have heard Mendelssohn's *S. Paul* will remember one of these hymns,

"Sleepers, wake, a voice is calling,"

with its fine chorale. This is another translation—

"Wake, wake ! for night is flying,
The watchmen on the heights are crying,
Awake, Jerusalem, at last.
Midnight hears the solemn voices,
And at the thrilling cry rejoices.
Come forth, ye virgins, night is past.
The Bridegroom comes, awake !
Your lamps with gladness take.
Hallelujah !
And for His marriage-feast prepare,
For ye must go and meet Him there."

The other hymn was composed by Nicolai when he was in great trouble. He was sitting thinking of all the misery and death around him, and then his spirit rose above this, and he thought of the love of Christ for us, and from the depths of his heart came this beautiful hymn. He forgot all that was going on, even his mid-day meal, and he did not rise until the hymn was finished. It begins—

> "O Morning Star, how fair and bright
> Thou beamest forth in truth and light,
> O Sovereign, meek and lowly."

This hymn and its tune became very popular ; it was often used at weddings, because of its allusion to the heavenly marriage-feast, and the tune rang out from city chimes.

Now we come to the Thirty Years' War (1618—1650). This was mainly one between the Roman and Reformed Church, and, as is always the case in religious wars, there was fearful suffering and persecution. But times of suffering often bring out men's best spiritual feelings, and certainly the hymns composed at this period were very fine. The star of German hymn-writers, Paul Gerhardt, lived at this time. He was pastor of S. Nicholas, a large church in Berlin, where he worked very hard, and was a very favourite preacher. Then the Elector published an edict, with which Gerhardt could not comply, so he was deprived of his living. Three of his children had died during their infancy, and now he lost one of his two remaining boys. On his death he wrote a most touching hymn—

> "Thou'rt mine, yes, still thou art mine own."

But his greatest trouble was his dear wife's sickness. She fell into a decline, and during this time he wrote many of his most beautiful hymns, which speak of the sorrow and the crosses he had to bear, yet how he rose above them to earnest trust in God.

A story is told about one of the most famous of Gerhardt's hymns, made known to English people by John Wesley's translation.   Paul had been banished from Berlin, and was wandering about with his wife and children, not knowing where to go.   One day he turned with his family into a small wayside inn.   His wife was very low and depressed, and to comfort her he repeated Psalm xxxvii. 5 : "Commit thy way unto the Lord, and put thy trust in Him, and He shall bring it to pass." Then they went out into the garden together, and sat under an apple-tree, and there he composed the hymn.

> "Commit thou all thy griefs
>   And ways into His hands ;
> To His sure truth and tender care,
>   Who heaven and earth commands."

The story goes on to relate how, that very evening, messengers arrived to offer Gerhardt a post of distinction under the Duke of Merseburg.

A very pretty custom was kept up in some of the high schools of Germany, that, when pupils left, their companions went with them to the gates of the town, singing this hymn, and thus committing them to the sure protection of their Heavenly Father.

One of Gerhardt's finest hymns was a translation from the Latin of S. Bernard's famous Passion hymn, and from the German is taken our translation—

"O sacred Head, surrounded."   (A. & M., 111.)

Many other hymns by Gerhardt are given in *Lyra Germanica;* one is a prayer for the nation, written during the Thirty Years' War, and there are two beautiful morning and evening hymns, the latter being much used by German children—

> "Now all the woods are sleeping,
> And night and stillness creeping
> O'er field and city, man and beast ;
> But thou, my heart, awake thee,
> To prayer awhile betake thee,
> And praise thy Maker ere thou rest." [1]

Gerhardt died in 1676, and his last words were from one of his own hymns—

> "Me no death hath power to kill."

His hymns have lived because they are so full of feeling and sympathy, and because the language is so simple, and pure, and earnest. They have been translated into many languages, and we read that Schwartz, a great Indian missionary, was comforted on his death-bed by hearing native Christians sing some of Gerhardt's hymns in their own language.

One of Paul Gerhardt's friends and patronesses was Louisa Henrietta, Electress of Brandenburg, a noble Christian lady, and the granddaughter of Admiral Coligny. She was married at the age of nineteen, and her firstborn son was taken from her, to her own and her husband's deep sorrow. Her charity was unbounded ; she founded schools and orphanages, and the people became so devoted to her that her portrait hung on almost every cottage wall, and *Louisa* became the favourite name for girls. But one thing weighed upon her mind : she had no other child, until at last her prayers were

---

[1] *Lyra Germanica,* 51.

answered, and a little son was born to her. She was very fond of reading and singing hymns, and made a collection of them. She also composed them, and the most celebrated is her favourite Easter hymn—

> "Jesus, my Redeemer, lives !
>   Christ, my trust, is dead no more;
>   In the strength this knowledge gives,
>   Shall not all my fears be o'er,
>   Though the night of Death be fraught
>   Still with many an anxious thought?"[1]

This was written after the death of her first little son, in 1649. In gratitude for her second child, she founded an orphan house at Oranienburg.

There were many other hymn-writers at this time. To Heinrich Albert (1644) we owe a beautiful morning hymn—

> "God, Who madest earth and heaven,
>   Father, Son, and Holy Ghost;
>   Who the day and night hast given,
>   Sun, and moon, and starry host;
>   All things wake at Thy command,
>   Held in being by Thy hand."[2]

Simon Dach, a friend of Albert, and Professor of Poetry in the University of Königsberg, wrote some beautiful hymns on the sufferings of Christians on earth.

> "Wouldst thou inherit life with Christ on high?
>   Then count the cost, and know
>   That here on earth below
>   Thou needst must suffer with thy Lord, and die.
>   We reach that gain to which all else is loss,
>   But through the Cross."[3]

---

[1] *Lyra Germanica.* Tuesday in Easter week.
[2] *Lyra Germanica*, 15.   [3] *Ibid.*, 812.

Another famous hymn of this period was

"Leave God to order all thy ways," [1]

by George Neumark. A baker's boy used to sing it at his work, and the people flocked to hear him, until it became carried all over the country.

Then we come to a rather different class of hymns, less simple, and more full of imagery. They speak much of the love of Christ, and of the soul's longing to be like Christ. Johann Franck, a burgomaster, wrote, about the year 1711, a beautiful hymn for Easter Eve—

> "So rest, my Rest,
> Thou ever blest,
> Thy grave with sinners making;
> By Thy precious death from sin
> My dead soul awaking.

> Here Thou hast lain,
> After much pain,
> Life of my life, reposing;
> Round Thee now a rock-hewn grave,
> Rock of Ages, closing.

> Breath of all Breath!
> I know from death
> Thou wilt my dust awaken.
> Wherefore should I dread the grave,
> Or my faith be shaken?" etc.

Franck also made a beautiful translation of S. Ambrose's famous hymn (A. & M., 55).

Angelus Silesius was another great poet of the time. His hymns breathe profound love to Christ. One is well known—

> "O Love, Who formedst me to wear."
> (Ch. Hy., 456 ; A. & M., 192.)

---

[1] *Lyra Germanica.* Thirteenth Sunday after Trinity.

Johann Herrmann, who lived a little later, wrote his beautiful Passion hymns when he was not only suffering from bodily disease, but was in danger from perils of war. More than once he only escaped being killed by a miracle. A beautiful story is told about one of his hymns, written to be sung " in time of war "—

"It was in the depth of winter, January 5, 1814, when, during a war, the enemy entered the town of Schleswig. Close by the entrance to the town, in a little cottage, there lived a poor widow, with her daughter and her grandson. The night before that fatal 5th the boy was reading to his grandmother out of his hymn-book, and he came to this hymn of Hermann's, one of the verses containing the line—

'A wall about us build,'

and when the boy came to it, he stopped, and said, ' It would be a good thing, grandmother, if our Lord God would build a wall around us.' They went to bed in fear and trembling, knowing that the next day might be their last ; but though cries of misery and distress were heard all through the town, before their door all was still. A terrific snowstorm had come on during the night, and strange to say, God had built a wall round them ; for a snowdrift had concealed them from the enemy's view, and in the midst of the anguish and terror in the city, they remained unharmed."

We come now to a very famous hymn—one that has been often called the " Te Deum of Germany." The war had gone on for years, and at last there seemed a prospect of a general peace. In the town of Eilenburg, in Saxony, there lived a good pastor, Martin Rinkart. Early in the month of November 1648, he sat at his study window, reading, when he heard the sound of a trumpet. His first thought was that soldiers were coming to devastate the town, but on going out into the

streets, he found the people weeping, not for
sorrow, but for joy. The trumpeter had brought
the joyful news that peace had been made, and
that the Thirty Years' War was over. Rinkart went
back into his study to pray, and praise God, and
opening his Bible, his eye fell upon these words—
" Now, therefore, bless ye the Lord God of all,
which only doeth wondrous things " (Ecclus. l. 22).
An angel seemed to guide his hand as he sat down
and wrote out the inspired hymn—

> " Now thank we all our God,
> With heart, and hands, and voices,
> Who wondrous things hath done,
> In Whom His world rejoices."
> (Ch. Hy., 439 ; A. & M., 379.)

Then, as he wrote the last line, a melody seemed
to fall upon his ear, as if the angels had lent it to
him from heaven, and he wrote that out also. He
went out into the public square, where the people
were gathered together, rejoicing with one another,
and kneeling down, he began to sing that wonderful
hymn, which, with its grand chorale, has been sung
at so many public thanksgivings for the last three
centuries, and which Mendelssohn has worked
with such great effect into his *Hymn of Praise.*
Rinkart, though not a soldier, like Gustavus
Adolphus, was as true a hero. A fearful plague
had devastated the country, and he visited and
cheered the poor people, and buried more than
four thousand of them ; and then, during the
famine which followed the plague, he helped the
poor sufferers as much as possible.

A story is told about this grand hymn of Rinkart's
by the American poet, Russell Lowell. A dreadful

fire had broken out in Hamburg, and had spread to the tower of the beautiful old church of S. Nicholas, from which the chimes rang out, at certain times of the day, the fine chorale composed by Rinkart to his hymn. An old verger, named Herrmann, had charge of these chimes, and like many another hero, died at the post of duty.

"Up in his tower old Herrmann sat, and watched with quiet look,
His soul had trusted God too long to be at last forsook ;
He could not fear, for surely God his pathway would unfold,
Through this Red Sea, for faithful hearts, as once he did of old.

Upon the peril's desperate peak his heart stood up sublime,
His first thought was for God alone, his next was for his chime ;
'Sing now, and make your voices heard in hymns of praise,' cried he,
As did the Israelites of old, safe walking through the sea.

Through the Red Sea our God hath made the pathway safe to shore,
Our promised land stands full in sight, shout now as ne'er before ; '
And as the tower came crashing down, the bells, in clear accord,
Pealed forth the grand old German hymn, 'All good souls praise the Lord.'"

We must not forget the fine hymn composed by Lowenstein, during the Thirty Years' War, and translated by Philip Pusey—

"Lord of our life, and God of our salvation."
(Ch. Hy., 269 ; A. & M., 214.)

XV.

GERMAN HYMNS.

EIGHTEENTH AND NINETEENTH CENTURIES.

"The devil, that lost spirit, cannot endure sacred songs of joy. Our passions and impatiences, our complainings and our cryings, our 'Alas !' and our 'Woe is me !' please him well ; but our songs and psalms vex and grieve him sorely."—LUTHER.

A GREAT hymn-writer of the early part of the eighteenth century was Gerhardt Tersteegen, a ribbon manufacturer at Mühlheim. He lived alone, had very simple habits, and gave away a great deal of money. He spent a great deal of his working time in meditation and prayer, and people used to come and talk to him, or send for him to read and pray with the sick. His hymns show his love of God and his childlike spirit. He used to say, "Father, I love most to be with Thee, but I am glad to be with Thy children." One of his beautiful hymns is given in *Lyra Germanica*, for the Holy Innocents' Day—

> "Dear Soul, couldst thou become a child,
> While yet on earth, meek, undefiled,
> Then God Himself were ever near,
> And Paradise around thee here."

In the same book is a lovely little evening hymn—

> "The day expires,
> My soul desires
> And pants to see that day,
> When the vexing cares of earth
> Shall be done away.

> The night is here,
> Oh, be Thou near,
> Christ, make it light within ;
> Drive away from out my heart
> All the night of sin." etc.

Two of our harvest hymns are from German sources. That for a deficiency in the crops—

> "What our Father does is well" (A. & M., 389),

written by Schmolck, a pastor in Silesia, who died in 1737, and translated by Sir Henry Baker ; and the very popular hymn—

> "We plough the fields, and scatter"
> (Ch. Hy., 282 ; A. & M., 383),

translated by Miss Campbell from a hymn by Matthias Claudius, born in Schleswig-Holstein in 1740. This appeared first in a tale by the author, called *Paul Erdmann's Fest.*

Another of our favourites, the All Saints' hymn—

> "Who are these like stars appearing"
> (Ch. Hy., 554 ; A. & M., 427),

translated by Miss Cox, was written by Heinrich Theobald Schenk, a school-master, who died in 1727. The original hymn contains fourteen verses.

Now we come to a celebrated Easter hymn, sung, in its translated form, almost as much in England as in Germany—

> "Jesus lives ! no longer now
> Can thy terrors, death, appal us."
> (A. & M., 140.)

Its author was Christian Fürchtegott Gellert, born in 1715 at Haynichen, in Saxony. He studied at Leipzig, intending to be a pastor ; but he was too modest and retiring to preach, and became a tutor and professor in the University. At one time the poet Goethe was among his pupils. While he was at Leipzig a war broke out, and there was fearful distress and poverty in the city. Gellert could not bear to see his fellow-creatures suffer, and he gave them so much of his small means that he was reduced to great straits himself. One winter morning, as he was going out into the country for a walk, he saw a poor woman sitting by the roadside, sobbing bitterly. He found that, owing to her husband's illness, she and her family were without food, and the landlord threatened to turn them out of their little home if the rent was not paid that very day. The money owing was thirty thalers, and Gellert possessed the exact sum ; but it was all he had, and he had saved it to buy firewood for the winter. The poor woman's need was greater than his own, so he gave her the money, and then went to the landlord, made him see how hard he was, so that he refused to take the poor woman's money, and she was able to take it for food. Next day Gellert began to feel the piercing cold and to realize the sacrifice he had made. He became chillier and chillier, so that the power nearly went out of his fingers ; and then he took up his Bible, found the Book of Job, and read ch. ii. 10 : "What ? shall we receive good at the hand of God, and shall we not receive evil ?" Then he took up his pen, and as fast as his blue fingers would allow him, he wrote the famous hymn—

"I have had my days of blessing,
All the joys of life possessing,
Unnumbered they appear.

> Then let faith and patience cheer me,
> Now that trials gather near me.
> Where is life without a tear?"[1]

He had just finished writing this, when a friend of his, a good doctor, came in, noticed how cold the room was, saw the hymn, and soon found out the whole story, not from Gellert himself, but from the poor woman he had helped. The doctor had to go to a farmhouse to see a patient, and there he found some Prussian officers sitting at dinner. One of them, who turned out to be Prince Henry of Prussia, inquired after Gellert, upon which the doctor told the story and produced the hymn. The story soon spread, and the farmer sent off a great load of firewood to Gellert, saying it was a present for a hymn. The old landlord, too, was touched, and sent back the thirty thalers, without any name, to the poet; and lastly, Prince Henry himself called upon him, thanked him for his hymn, and gave him a valuable present. Gellert died at Leipzig in 1767, having held the Professorship of Poetry and Philosophy there, and written many books and much sacred poetry.

Three beautiful hymns, translated by Miss Jane Borthwick, in *Hymns from the Land of Luther*, were written about this time. One by Spitta, for lay helpers—

> " How blessed, from the bonds of sin."
> (Ch. Hy., 300 ; A. M., 357).

A fine and spirited Advent hymn, by Laurenti, who died in 1722—

> " Rejoice, all ye believers,
> And let your lights appear ;

---

[1] Translated in *Hymns from the Land of Luther*.

The evening is advancing,
And darker night is near.
The Bridegroom is arising,
And soon He draweth nigh ;
Up, pray, and watch, and wrestle,
At midnight comes the cry."
(Hymn. Comp., 70.)

The most beautiful of the three is the morning hymn, by Knorr von Rosenroth, who died in 1689—

"Jesu, Sun of Righteousness,
Brightest beam of Love Divine,
With the early morning rays
Do Thou on our darkness shine,
And dispel with purest light
All our night."   (Hymn. Comp., 7.)

Another pretty little hymn, by the same translator, is from the German of Krummacher (1767—1845), and is given in a story of his of the festal dedication of a village church, destroyed in time of war, sung by boys and girls after the celebration of Holy Communion—

"Yes, our Shepherd leads with gentle hand
Through the dark pilgrim land,
His flock so dearly bought,
So long and fondly sought.   Alleluia ! "
(Children's Hy. Bk., 188.)

Now we come to the Moravian hymns, from which John and Charles Wesley took so many of their best known hymns. The Moravians were descendants of the Bohemian Brethren, followers of John Huss, in the fifteenth century, and had their chief settlement at Fulnek, in Moravia. They were very earnest, pious people, and great missionaries. There was a certain Count von Zinzendorf, a nobleman of great wealth, who joined the Moravian sect during the eighteenth century.   He was passing one day through the picture gallery at Düsseldorf, when he saw a painting of our Saviour, crowned with thorns, with the words inscribed on it—

> "All this have I done for thee,
> What doest thou for Me?"

This had so much effect upon the Count that he resolved to devote his life to God and to work for Him.   He became a great missionary, and founded Moravian settlements in America, England, and other countries.   Amongst other things, he wrote no less than 2000 hymns.   One, translated by Miss Winkworth, is well known—

> "Christ will gather in His own."
>   (Ch. Hy., 244 ; A. & M., 400.)

Another, very beautiful, given in the Hymn. Comp. (17), is—

> "Jesu, still lead on,
> Till our rest be won,
> And, although the way be cheerless,
> We will follow, calm and fearless ;
> Guide us by Thy Hand,
> To our Fatherland."

John Wesley formed a great friendship with Zinzendorf, and took many of his ideas about hymns from the Moravians, who used them a great deal in their worship.   The modern German hymns and writers are too numerous to name, and we will only mention one or two of the best known—

> "When morning gilds the skies " (A. & M., 303),

translated by the Rev. E. Caswall, from a German hymn of unknown authorship, of the eighteenth or nineteenth century. Another favourite hymn for mourners, by Schenk (*b.* 1751)—

> "O let him whose sorrow
> No relief can find."
> (Ch. Hy., 471 ; A. & M., 286.)

Two other translations we owe to Miss Winkworth, a baptismal hymn, written by a pastor named Albert Knapp (*d.* 1864), for the baptism of his own children—

> "O Father, Thou Who hast created all";

and the beautiful hymn for the Burial of a Child—

> "Tender Shepherd, Thou hast stilled."
> (Ch. Hy., 249 ; A. & M., 402.)

This was written by a Lutheran pastor, named Meinhold (*d.* 1851), after the death of one of his own children. In his poems it is headed : "Sung in four parts beside the body of my little fifteen-months-old son, Johannes Ladislaus." It may also be interesting to know that Dr. Dykes, who had long been anxious to write a tune for this hymn, and had never before been able to satisfy himself, composed a beautiful tune just after the death of his youngest daughter Mabel, from scarlet fever, at the age of ten years. This was sung at her funeral, so both words and music were inspired by personal feeling, and written under very touching circumstances.

XVI.

FRENCH HYMNS.

" O bien heureux qui voir pourra
Fleurir le temps que l'on vira,
Le laboureur à sa charrue,
Le charretier parmi la rue,
Et l'artisan en sa boutique,
Aveques une Psaume ou Cantique
En son labeur se soulager."—CLEMENT MAROT.

ALTHOUGH French literature is so famous, the field of French hymnody is not nearly so large as that of Germany. Indeed, we can hardly trace any hymns before the sixteenth century, although several of the carols still used are very old, and are found in different *patois*, which shows that there may have been hymns like them. Breton carols, especially, were very numerous ; and we hear, in very early times, of the blind Breton poet, Hervé, who became the head of a small monastic school, and used to teach his pupils sacred songs and hymns of this sort—

"Approach, my little children ; come and hear a new song which I have composed expressly for you—take pains to remember it entirely. When you awake in your bed, offer your heart to the good God; make the sign of the cross, and say with faith, hope, and love, 'My God, I give Thee my body and my soul, make me to be a good man, or else to die before my time.' When you see a raven fly, think that the devil is as black and wicked ; when you see a little white dove fly, think that your angel is as sweet and white."

Until the sixteenth century, only Latin hymns were used in the Church services ; but France,

like Germany, had her great outburst of song at
the Reformation, and the first hymns, or, rather,
metrical psalms, we have to speak of are those
sung by the persecuted Huguenots in the fifteenth
and sixteenth centuries, and chiefly written by
Clement Marot, a great Huguenot psalmist. He
was born at a little French town called Cahors-
sur-Quercy, and spent the first ten years of his
life there. The town stands upon a rock, round
three sides of which a river winds, and the people
still show an oak under which the gifted boy used
to sit. His father, Jean Marot, had the same
talent, and in the year 1506 became poet to Anne
of Brittany, second wife of Louis XII., and
brought his wife and child to settle in Paris.
Jean was a good man, and his boy, trained at
Court, became honest, thoughtful, and poetical.
Anne died in 1514, but Marot still remained at
Court, encouraging his son's poetic genius, and
teaching him in the long evenings. Then Clement
went to the wars with Francis I., who was about
the same age as himself, and afterwards was
made valet in the house of Marguerite, Duchesse
d'Alençon, a beautiful and clever woman, who took
great interest in the Reformation. After Jean
Marot died, with his son's hand in his, Clement
went forth to fight again. He was made prisoner
at the battle of Pavia, and the rest of his life was a
series of adventures and imprisonments. While
in prison he wrote much poetry, and even during
severe illness he was bright and cheerful, and
"poured forth in verse his creeds, his prayers,
and grace before and after meat." After being
exiled and condemned to the stake, Marot, after

many adventures, took refuge at Lyons, and then began to turn the Psalms of David into verse.

When, on New Year's Day, 1540, Charles V. and Francis I. rode into Paris side by side, Clement presented to Charles the thirty psalms he had then translated. Before this time they had been dark enigmas to the people ; now, in their own language and in easy rhyme, they were clear to all.

A little book, printed in 1542, contains " The form of prayer in French churches and French hymns." Among the hymns are Marot's thirty psalms, which were soon set to popular airs, and became fashionable both at Court and in cottage. Children sang them at play, and for three centuries they have been household words to the Huguenots and their descendants in France and Switzerland. Clement died at Turin in 1544. His motto still lives—" *La mort n'y mort.*"

"Among the poets, Clement Marot, whether he sung of human or Divine love, whether in jest or prayer, always expressed in simple and fit words thoughts suitable to the occasion. He wrote like a good Frenchman, generous, courteous, loving France, fame, fair ladies ; *but God above them all.*"

At the request of Calvin, Marot's *Psalter* was afterwards finished, and published in 1552, and became most popular. The Huguenots used special psalms for special occasions—for instance, Psalm iii. for the stationing of sentinels to guard against sudden attack, because of the verse, " I will not be afraid for ten thousands of the people, that have set themselves against me round about." And then, when danger was over, and they could worship again in peace, they would sing Psalm

cxxii., " O, pray for the peace of Jerusalem." But
the most celebrated of Marot's psalms was the
sixty-eighth, sung before many a battle—" Let
God arise," etc.

> " Que Dieu se montre seulement
> Et l'on verra dans un moment,
> Abandonner la place ;
> Le camp des ennemis épars,
> Epouvanté de toutes parts,
> Fuira devant sa face."

In 1589, Henri IV., the great Huguenot leader,
was overtaken by the Roman Catholic party at
Dieppe, and his small force nearly crushed by
the hostile power. " Come," said the king, " lift
the psalm ; it is full time." And the battle-song
of Marot rolled out from those brave men—

> " Let God arise, and let His enemies be scattered."

" Slowly moving along, the two companies split the armies
of the leaguers. The swing of the psalm was tuned to the
long roll of the guns, and then, strange to say, the fog which
had come in from the sea lifted—hung around and above
them as they sang, ' Like as the mist vanisheth, so shalt
Thou drive them away,' and the leaguers were scattered."

Again, at the siege of La Rochelle, the same
psalm was sung. Huguenot fugitives had fled
from all parts to this rocky fortress ; it was
occupied by 1600 citizens and 1500 strangers, and
in 1572 the royal army was sent to besiege it.

" The fort was well provisioned and garrisoned, and after
battering the walls for five weeks, with no success, the
enemy determined upon a regular assault. Four attempts
were made, and four times the battle-song resounded from
the towers, and the besiegers were driven back, though on
both sides there was fearful loss of life. The women helped
to drive away the besiegers by mounting the walls and

pouring down boiling tar and stones on them. In the month of June the fort was still not taken, though food had run short ; but the Huguenots managed to get some shell-fish from the bay, which kept them alive until the siege was raised and peace restored."

Smith says that this sixty-eighth Psalm was the Marseillaise of the Camisards,[1] their war-song in many battles; and that when it was sung, each soldier became a lion in courage. Once, when the Camisards were attacked, they received the first fire of the soldiers on one knee, singing—

" Que Dieu se montre seulement."

Singing was certainly a great power among these persecuted people, and their enemies knew it, and at certain times during the struggle the singing of psalms was forbidden, on land or water, in workshops or dwellings, under pain of death.

Once, during a lull in the persecutions in Paris, in 1558, thousands of people assembled to listen to psalms, sung by men of " The Religion," as they marched along. One of the favourites among Marot's psalms was the fourth, sung as an evening hymn, and also at funerals—

" Si qu'en paix et sureté bonne,
    Coucherai et reposerai,
    Car 'Seigneur, ta bonté tout ordonne
    Et elle seule espoir, me donne,
    Que sûr et seul regnant serai."
" I will lay me down in peace and take my rest," etc.

We might give many more instances of the way these psalms were sung, but we must pass on to the hymns of the Roman Church. The great

[1] A band of Huguenots.

French poets, Racine and Corneille, each left some sacred songs or hymns amongst their poetry. Corneille versified the *Imitation of Christ*, and some parts of this have been used as hymns, and are found in most collections. Then Fénélon, like Ephrem of old, composed some hymns, in the hope of replacing the wicked ballads used at Court ; and he repeated one of his own hymns on his death-bed.

We come next to a celebrated name, that of Madame Guyon (1648—1717), the leader of a religious movement called the Quietist Movement. She married very early, when only sixteen, M. Guyon, a rich man, of weak health, who was twenty-two years older than herself, and their married life was very unhappy. He died in 1686, and then she began to try and spread abroad her doctrines, which gave great offence in some quarters. Madame Guyon came to Paris, and there she was taken up and imprisoned for her opinions in a convent of Faubourg S. Antoine ; but, after eight months, she was released. Then she rose to the height of her fame, and many of the Court, with Fénélon and the Ladies of the College of S. Cyr, came under the spell of her doctrine and holy life. She was again imprisoned, and not released till 1702, after which she spent the rest of her life in retirement, with her daughter, the Marquise de Vaux, at Blois. She died in full communion with the Roman Catholic Church.

Her writings fill forty volumes ; she wrote a great many hymns, but they were much more suitable for private than public use, and many were written when she was in prison, or when ill in bed. She often wrote as many as five or six a

day, and she believed that they were directly inspired by God rather than composed by herself,
and nearly all were upon the *Love* of God. There
were nearly 900 of these *Cantiques Spirituels*, and
in 1782 our poet Cowper translated thirty-seven of
them into English. This is a verse of one—

> "I love my God, but with no love of mine,
>   For I have none to give ;
> I love Thee, Lord, but all the love is Thine,
>   For by Thy life I live.
> I am as nothing, and rejoice to be
> Emptied, and lost, and swallowed up in Thee."

To return to the hymns of the French Reformed
Church. In 1705, fifty-four hymns were added to
Marot's *Psalter*, and soon became popular. One
was the Christmas hymn which has been so well
translated by Bishop Jenner—

> "Christians, sing out with exultation." (A. & M., 484.)

But the greatest French hymn-writer was Cæsar
Malan, of Geneva, who gave the first impulse to
hymn-singing in public worship. There was a
movement called the *Réveil*, or awakening, something like that of the Wesleys in our country at
the early part of this century, and Malan's hymns,
with his own melodies, did much to help the movement. His family came from the valleys of Pied-
mont, but were driven, by persecution, to Geneva ;
and here, in 1787, the poet was born. His hymns
are still widely used, and we know his name best
by one found in many hymn-books—

> "It is not death to die ;
>   To leave this weary road,
> And 'mid the brotherhood on high
>   To be at home with God.

Jesus, Thou Prince of Life !
Thy chosen cannot die ;
Like Thee, they conquer in the strife
To reign with Thee on high."

We must not forget the two devoted pastors of the Alps—Felix Neff (1798—1829) and Oberlin, both hymn-writers ; and Jacques Bridaine (1701—1767), a celebrated preacher, also gave us the hymn so beautifully translated by the Rev. T. B. Pollock—

" My Lord, my Master, at Thy feet adoring." (A. & M., 494.)

XVII.

ITALIAN HYMNS.

" For all we know
Of what the blessed do above,
Is that they *sing*—and that they *love*."

ALTHOUGH Italy was renowned in the Middle Ages as the country of music and poetry, and though we have seen what famous Latin hymn-writers she produced, it is known that there was no writing in the Italian language before the thirteenth century. In the early part of that century (1182—1225) lived one whose saintly life of voluntary poverty has made his name a household word amongst us, S. Francis of Assisi, who turned his gift of song to the glory of God.

In his early days he used to roam about the streets of his native town with his fellow-troubadours, singing songs of love and war, soft serenades, and romantic ballads. When he was about twenty-five he resolved to give himself and all that he had to God, and to live a life of poverty and self-denial. His father, a rich merchant, cast him off, and he went out into the snow-covered hills and wintry woods —a pilgrim bereft of every earthly thing. But as he wandered, not knowing where he went, the pilgrim lifted his voice and sang. "In the heart of Italy, through the crackling, leafless woods, with nothing on him but his hair-shirt covered with a peasant's frock, the visionary went singing God's praises in the gay tongue of France." It is said that he met robbers, who, startled by his singing, threw him into a snow-drift; but at this he only rejoiced, praising God yet louder.

Although S. Francis sang in French, the language of the troubadours, he wrote his hymns afterwards in Italian. He was soon joined by companions, who went about with him preaching and collecting alms, and one of them helped him with the songs he wrote to the praise and glory of God. About the year 1224, S. Francis spent forty nights in his prayers and vigils, after which he desired one of the brothers to write, and chanted what is called the Canticle of the Sun, or the Song of the Creatures. It is a song of praise from creation, not unlike the fine medieval hymn "The strain upraise," although the rhythm is not so exact. It is a curious, irregular hymn, but it describes the man and his intensely loving feelings to God and to Nature—

"Great God of all, omnipotent and high,
To Thee be glory, honour, laud, and praise,
And blessing, Lord, we raise ;
We are not worthy e'en Thy Name to say.

Praise be to God the Lord,
From creatures one and all,
From Brother Sun, our Lord,
Who lights us by his rays,
And radiant makes the days.
All glory to the Lord be given.

Praise be to God my Lord,
From Sister Moon, so fair and bright,
And from the stars that make the darkness light.
Praise be to God our Lord,
From Brother Wind, from clouds and air,
From weather dull and fair.
Praise be to God the Lord,
From Sister Water, chaste and pure,
So precious, useful and demure.
Praise be to God my Lord,
From Brother Fire, gay, robust and strong,
Who sparkles merrily the whole night long.
Praise be to God for our dear mother-earth,
In whom all fruits and flowers have their birth."

This was the original song, but two more verses were added on separate occasions. The first was this:—There had been a quarrel between the Bishop of Assisi and the magistrates of the town, so great that the Bishop had put the town under an interdict, and the magistrates had outlawed the Bishop. The tender, loving heart of Francis was grieved by this, and he determined to try and make peace. So he asked the people of the town to meet at the Bishop's palace, and when they arrived his disciples broke forth singing the new verse of the canticle he had made for the occasion—

" Praise be to God my Lord,
By those who, pardoning, suffer and are strong,
And meekly bear, for Thy Sake, shame and wrong.
Blessed are those who glory in Thy Love,
For Thou shalt crown them, Lord, on high above."

We read that when the song, with its new verse,
fell on their ears, their hearts smote them ; they
embraced each other and made up the quarrel.
They were taken by storm, and Francis's victory
was complete.

The last verse of all is, perhaps, still more touching. S. Francis had been ill. In the midst of his
suffering and weakness he had a vision which told
him that in two years' time his sufferings would be
ended, and he should enter into rest. Then he
added the last verse —

" Praise be to God for our dear Sister Death,
    From whom no living man can run or fly :
    Woe ! woe to them in mortal sin who die ;
    Blessed be they who in Thy Holy Will spend the last
        hour ;
    On them the second death shall have no power.
    Praise, thanks and blessing to our Master be,
    Serve ye Him all, with great humility."

Several other hymns, written either by S. Francis
or his disciples, have come down to us. One is
nearly certainly by him. Each verse begins and
ends, " Love sets my heart on fire "—

        " My heart breaks with desire,
        Love sets my heart on fire."

In the cities of Northern Italy, people had been
accustomed to listen in the public places to the
songs of *jongleurs*, or travelling musicians ; and
about the year 1250, Giacomo of Verona, like S.
Aldhelm at Sherborne, composed religious poems
in the Veronese dialect, which were sung to the
people as they sat in the piazzas. These were
chiefly about the terror of the Inferno, the glory
and beauty of the heavenly Jerusalem. In the

latter part of the thirteenth century appeared the Flagellants, enthusiasts who led large processions of men, women, and children from city to city, girded with ropes and scourging themselves, singing hymns and chanting prayers. Then Jacopone, the author of the celebrated Latin hymn, *Stabat Mater*, wrote Italian hymns. He was put into prison for denouncing the wickedness of the age, and especially the wrong-doings of the Popes, and he employed himself, like so many other prisoners, by composing hymns, which soon became popular.

We come next to a great name, that of Savonarola. Like so many other great reformers, he not only *preached* to the people, but used the means of sacred song to denounce the vice and luxury of the time. Lorenzo de Medici had written some carnival songs, which were much sung by the young nobles, and were most profane and wicked. In order to counteract their influence, Savonarola composed sacred songs or hymns, of the same metre, and set to the same tunes, for the people to . sing. He began by trying to reform the *children*.

"Foreseeing that it would be extremely difficult to entirely abolish the old customs, he decided to transform them by substituting religious for carnival gaieties. Accordingly, at the same street-corners where the children formerly assembled to demand money for their bouquets, he caused small altars to be erected, before which they were to take their stand, and beg contributions, not, however, for purposes of self-indulgence, but for alms to the poor. 'Sing as much as ye will,' he said to the boys, 'but sing hymns and sacred lauds instead of indecent songs.' Then Palm Sunday being at hand, he arranged a very edifying and solemn procession for the children, first preaching a sermon to them, ending with these words : 'O Lord, from the mouths of these little ones shall Thy true praises proceed.'"

I

The hymns written by Savonarola for these festivals were not always very poetical, but all show great originality and elevation of thought, and became very popular. It is strange how often, at different periods of Church history, sacred hymns have been used to supplant wicked and blasphemous songs. There are now several collections of Italian hymns ; but for some time it was not considered right in the Roman Catholic Church to have hymns in the common language of the people, at any rate, during Mass. However, they are used now for special occasions, especially during missions, and during the month of May, when there are many services in honour of the Blessed Virgin. In North Italy there is a popular collection of hymns and songs called the *Catholic Lyra*, often sung by the peasants at work in the fields. The Waldensians have a hymn-book containing translations from well-known English and German hymns. The only hymn which we use translated from the Italian is a very beautiful Passion hymn, by an unknown author, probably of the eighteenth century—

" Viva, viva, Jesu."   " Glory be to Jesus."
(Ch. Hy., 369 ; A. & M., 107.)

XVIII.

HYMNS OF SCANDINAVIA AND HOLLAND.

" And where are kings and empires now,
Since then, that went and came?
But Holy Church is praying yet,
A thousand years the same !
And these that sing shall pass away,
New choirs their room shall fill ;
Be sure thy children's children here
Shall hear those anthems still."—BISHOP COXE.

UNTIL the Reformation, the churches of Denmark, Norway, Sweden, and Iceland used Latin
hymns only ; but as soon as the service began to be
said in the mother-tongue, hymns in the language
of the people were introduced. In Sweden, the
first hymn-writers were two renowned brothers,
Olaf and Lawrence Petersen, fellow-reformers with
the king, Gustavus Vasa. Besides original hymns,
they made many translations from the Latin and
German. Then, curiously enough, came two other
brothers, the Andersens, who published a hymn-
book in the year 1536, and the elder of whom,
Lawrence, brought out a Swedish edition of the
Bible.

In the same century we have two royal names
in the list of hymn-writers. One was the ill-
fated king, Erik, who died by poison in 1577, and
who left two hymns, one a paraphrase of Psalm li.
The other was the hero-king, Gustavus Adolphus
(1594—1632), a great and good man. He was
called " The Lion of the North," and was possessed
of the most wonderful calmness and serenity—

smiling, it is said, in the very thick of the battle. He appointed to each regiment a chaplain, who gathered the soldiers round them, while, bare-headed, they chanted their morning and evening prayer. No wonder that, with such a leader, they feared no foe. The battle-cry of Gustavus Adolphus was "God with us"; and after his victory at Leipsic, September 7, 1631, he wrote out roughly the sketch of a hymn. This he showed to his chaplain, Fabricius, who made it into regular verse; and it was published under the title, *A Heart-cheering Song of Comfort on the Watchword of the Evangelical Army in the Battle of Leipsic*—"God with us." Another chaplain, Altenburg, composed a chorale for the hymn, and it was sung continually by the army. These are the first and last verses, translated—

> "Fear not, O little flock, the foe,
>   Who madly seeks your overthrow;
>   Dread not his rage and power:
>   What though your courage sometimes faints,
>   His seeming triumph o'er God's saints
>   Lasts but a little hour.
> Amen, Lord Jesus, grant our prayer,
> Great Captain, now Thine arm make bare;
>   Fight for us once again!
> So shall Thy saints and martyrs raise
> A mighty chorus to Thy praise,
>   World without end. Amen." [1]

The account of the last time this hymn was used by the hero, at the battle of Lützen, is very touching—

"A severe wound prevented the king from putting on his armour that day; 'but,' said he, 'God is my armour.' In

---

[1] *Lyra Germanica*, 239.

the presence of the foe, while the morning mist hung over
the field, he commanded Luther's well-known psalm—'Ein
feste burg'—to be sung, and then his own hymn. The hymns
were accompanied by all the guns and trumpets of the whole
army. Immediately after the mist broke, and the sunshine
burst upon the two armies. Kneeling by his horse, he repeated his usual battle-prayer, 'O Lord Jesus Christ, bless
our arms and this day's battle, for the glory of Thy Holy
Name.' A few words of encouragement to his soldiers ; the
battle-cry, 'God with us '; and at the head of a regiment he
rushed at the enemy. His left arm was shattered by a pistol-
shot ; then, shot through the back, he fell from his horse. His
body was found by the Swedes, with seven fresh wounds and
the scars of thirteen more. Thus fell a man, a Christian, a
hero, a king."

During the next century there were a succession
of Swedish hymn-writers. Norway and Iceland
took their hymns chiefly from Denmark ; but the
sacred poetry of that country ranks almost as high
as that of Germany. Even as early as the year
1569, the Danish hymns were so numerous that
Bishop Thömison wrote a history of them, from
the beginning of the Reformation until that year.
Bishop Kingo re-edited the Danish hymn-book in
1689, and in the next year he published a beautiful
hymn on *Gethsemane.* Both hymn and tune were
very popular in Denmark—

> "Over Kedron Jesus treadeth,
> To His passion for us all."

One of Kingo's hymns is—

> "O Jesu, Blessed Lord, to Thee" (A. & M., 558) ;

and the well-known hymn,

> "Through the night of doubt and sorrow " (A. & M., 274),

is by Ingemann, a Danish poet (1789—1862), who
edited a new hymn-book, founded upon Kingo's,

with many new additions. There is no doubt that many other beautiful Danish hymns worthy of translation might be found.

The chief hymn-book used throughout the Lutheran North now is the *Danish and Norwegian Psalm-book*, which contains five hundred and sixty hymns, one of the most popular being

"Jesu, o'er Thy bleeding frame,
　Sad I ponder, full of woe ;
Stirs my soul with grief and shame,
　That my Lord should suffer so." etc.

A Danish princess, Leonora Christina, daughter of King Christian IV. of Denmark, who was unjustly imprisoned in the year 1663, became one of the many prisoner-hymnists. Pen and ink were denied her, but some one gave her a small piece of chalk, and she wrote her hymns on a board, wiping the words away as soon as it was full. Some of her hymns have been preserved and translated into English. One, for the morning—

"God's praise I will be singing,
　In every waking hour,
My grateful tribute bringing,
　To magnify His power,
　And His Almighty love.
His angel-watchers sending,
My couch with mercy tending,
　And watching from above."

One of the warders was very rude to the princess, and never ceased to torment and ridicule her. On Good Friday, 1667, his conduct had been particularly bad, and Leonora wrote on her board a hymn on the sufferings of Christ, which, unfortunately, has not been preserved. She used often to sing

this hymn to herself, and one day the man heard
the words, and they so softened his heart that he
asked her forgiveness. After twenty years of this
terrible life Leonora was released, and a royal
manor and yearly pension given her. Her daily
prayer was—" May the Lord help all prisoners ;
console the guilty, and save the innocent."

Holland has also its national hymnody. As
in other countries, Latin hymns were first used
there ; then, gradually, some came to be of mixed
Latin and Dutch ; and, after the Reformation,
though hymns at first were thought by the Calvin-
ists to be wrong, a collection of Psalter Songs was
published in 1539, and eagerly sung. After this
several other versions of the Psalter were made,
some being translations from the French of Marot
and Beza. One of these was by Peter Datheen,
a monk who renounced his vows and preached
Calvinism to very large crowds, who came round
him to hear his sermons, and sing psalms in the
open air.

In 1580, Philip van S. Aldegonde, who was
called "poet, orator, hymn-book maker, burgomaster, lawyer, and soldier," added to his version
of the Psalter some metrical versions of Bible
hymns, the Lord's Prayer, etc. In 1612 a rule
was made that hymns upon the Life of our Lord
might be used in public worship ; but these were
suppressed again, and it was really not until the
beginning of this century that the hymnal of the
Dutch Church was authorized. It contains many
beautiful hymns, few original, many from the German ; and much sung by the Boers, the Dutch
settlers in South Africa.

XIX.

WELSH HYMNS.

" Their Lord they will praise,
   Their speech they will keep,
   Their land they will lose,
      Except wild Wales."

" No musician is skilful unless he extols the Lord, and no
   singer is correct unless he praises the Father."--TALIESIN
   (a British bard of the sixth century, apropos of Welsh
   Hymns).

NOW we come to the corner of our kingdom where
Christianity was first planted, and where the
Alleluia victory was won. We see by the place-
names in Wales, many of which are very old, how
religion was the foundation, as it were, of all the
people did. How many begin with *Llan*, which
means " church " [1] ; and over and over again we find
Capel = " chapel," and *Merthyr* = " martyr." We
know that there were Christians in Wales in the
second century; and so, no doubt, where there were
Christians there were also Christian hymns, for
the Welsh have always been renowned for their
love of music.

Although we know that these early hymns
existed, and read of the fine voices of the ancient
Britons, we find no record of any till the year 1340,
when David Dhu, a canon of S. Asaph, composed
some Welsh hymns, and translated the Te Deum
and some psalms into Welsh metre. Then, at the
Reformation, the fire of song burst forth, as it did
in England and Germany, and other countries ; for,

---

[1] Originally " enclosure."

before that time, the Latin hymns had chiefly been
sung in the Welsh churches. In the year 1579,
Vicar Pritchard wrote what was called *The Welsh-
man's Candle*, a sort of Welsh hymn-book. He
was the first preacher of his day, and so popular,
that when he came into residence as a canon of S.
David's, he used a movable pulpit, which was put
into the churchyard, because the cathedral was
too small to hold the number of people who came
to hear him. Then, finding that his hearers were
fond of singing, he wisely turned the substance of
his sermons into verse, and so gave the Welsh
people some of their earliest hymns. In 1588
came the whole Bible, translated into Welsh, and
this gave a spur to the poets, and helped them to
write their sacred songs. Then, just before the
dawn of the seventeenth century, two poetical
versions of the Psalms into Welsh appeared. One
was by a soldier—Captain Williams Middleton,
one of those brave men who defended England from
the Spaniards. Captain Middleton, being a very
warlike man, seems to have liked best those psalms
which speak of the enemies of the Lord being
pursued. He translated these into Welsh, "keeping as near as he could to the mind of the Holy
Ghost"; but, sad to say, his metres were so hard
that no music would fit them, and his work proved
a failure on earth, though no doubt rewarded in
heaven. It was finished in the Island of Scutum,
in the West Indies, January 24, 1595. While
Middleton was far away from his beloved mountains, a countryman of his, Edward Kyffin, was
doing the same work at home, "for such of his
beloved countrymen as love the glory of the Lord

and the cherishing of their own mother-tongue."
He only put thirteen of the Psalms into verse,
hoping that it might be an inducement to others to
do the same.

In 1621 was published the complete Psalter of
Archdeacon Prys, who was accustomed to prepare
a psalm for each Sunday, in order, as he said,
"that the Welsh people might be enabled to praise
God from their hearts." His Psalter is one of the
chief treasures of Welsh hymnology, being sung
by the people, not only in service, but in the fields
or on the mountains. In some cases his rendering of a verse throws a flood of light upon its
meaning. A story is told about one verse. A
Roundhead preacher of the eighteenth century
went over to the Isle of Anglesey, and met with
great opposition there. The people declared that,
if he began to preach, they would kill him; but he
was a brave man, and did not fear them. So he
stood upon a rock ready to begin his sermon, while
the people began to come near him, threatening
him with their staves. Then, looking up into the
sky, he gave out this verse, to be sung with the few
who sided with him—

> "I lift mine eyes unto the hills,
>   Whence willing help shall come." (Ps. cxxi. 1, 2.)

The people, imagining that the preacher expected
some soldiers coming to rescue him, retreated.
Then some of them thought they would like to
hear what the good man had to say, unseen by
him; and one of them relates how the preacher
convinced him of his sin, and he became a devoted
follower of Christ.

Two poets, both named Vaughan, come next on our list. *Rowland* Vaughan's chief work was translating hymns into Welsh—amongst others, the *Veni Creator;* but he was a Royalist, and his love for the king brought him great sufferings. His house was burnt down by the Republicans, and his estates confiscated.

Henry Vaughan is well known as the author of many beautiful sacred poems, but we can hardly call him a hymn-writer.

A beautiful Welsh funeral hymn, which always appeared in the Welsh Prayer-book after the year 1710, was written by *Elis Wyn*, who was born near Harlech, in the year 1670. During the eighteenth century, a cattle-dealer, named David Jones, translated Dr. Watts' Psalms and Hymns into Welsh, and these became very popular. But William Williams was the *great* hymn-writer of Wales. He, like many great poets, was brought up in troublous times. His father was the deacon of an Independent Chapel, whose congregation had to hide in a cave, at twilight hour, for fear of their persecutors. Williams chose the profession of a doctor, and went to college. One Sunday morning he passed through a little village, and hearing the church bells ring, he went into church. The service was cold and dull, and made no impression on him; but, as he came out, he saw that the people were standing about, waiting for something, and presently a tall, dark-looking man stood up on one of the gravestones and began to preach. It was Whitfield, whose sermons were stirring up the Welsh to great religious enthusiasm. Williams was so much impressed by what he heard, that his whole life was altered, and two years later he was ordained deacon in the English Church. He became not only a great hymn-writer, but a great preacher, going about all over the country, as Whitfield did. Most of his hymns were written in his native language, and are, like most Welsh hymns, picturesque, speaking of rocks and mountains, valleys and brooks, of storm and sunshine, of wandering on dangerous narrow paths, of Nature and all her many moods. Once, during a long season of drought, Williams was walking through the fields and found some little animals making mischief among the green corn, and at once he turned this subject into a hymn. Another time, when he was staying near the Priscelly hills, he woke up early in the morning and saw the hills lying dark and gloomy under the mist, while, in the east, the dawn was breaking and the sky brightening. So he brought this picture into his missionary hymn—

" O'er the gloomy hills of darkness."

But the hymn we know best, by Williams, in its translation from the Welsh original, is—

" Guide me, O Thou great Redeemer."
(Ch. Hy., 376 ; A. & M., 196.)

He wrote over eight hundred hymns, which, like those of Wesley in England, did more than anything else to rouse the people of Wales from the dull sleep into which they had fallen. Williams died in 1791, and is buried in a quiet village churchyard in a Welsh valley.

Another hymn-writer was David Williams, a school-master. He had a wife whose temper was a great trial to him. One stormy night he came home from a preaching tour, and his wife's tongue was raging with such vehemence that he preferred the storm outside to that within the house. So he went to stand by the river, and the rush of its waters reminded him of another mighty river, the river of Death, and he sang—

> " In the waves and mighty waters
> No one will support my head,
> But my Saviour, my Beloved,
> Who was stricken in my stead :
> In the cold and mortal river,
> He will hold my head above ;
> I shall through the waves go singing,
> For one look of Him I love."

This is generally called the miners' hymn, and a very touching incident is connected with it. In the month of April 1877, a colliery in Wales was flooded. All know what *that* means ; what anguish to wife, mother, and child, knowing that the men and boys who went down in the morning may be drowned or suffocated before night sets in. Fourteen of the miners were in a dark prison below ; safe for a time from the water, but hourly expecting death from starvation or want of air. The rescue-party toiled day and night to release them ; but seven long days passed, and they had not been found. On the eighth day nine of the men were found at the point of death, having been without air or food for a long time. When they recovered and were able to tell their story, they said that despair would have driven them mad had it not been for the miners' hymn, which they sang over and over again.

There have been no great Welsh hymn-writers

since the last century, for the English language is
now so freely spoken that there is not the same
occasion for Welsh hymns. The last writer we can
name was a farmer's daughter, named Ann Griffiths,
born 1776. She used to repeat her hymns as she
composed them to a servant named Ruth, and the
two sang them together. After her mistress's
death, Ruth wrote them down, and they were afterwards published, and are now much used in Wales.

Whether or no it is a fact that mountainous
countries are musical, we are certain that, ever
since the days of the bards, the Welsh have excelled
in music and harmony. Even now it is the custom
to sing hymns or psalms on the way to funerals,
and the powerful voices of the men peal across glen
and mountain, as they carry the body to its last
resting-place.

XX.

ENGLISH HYMNS.

THE SIXTEENTH AND SEVENTEENTH CENTURIES.

"A verse may find him whom a sermon flies,
And turn delight into a sacrifice."—G. HERBERT.

WE come now to the sixteenth century in England, the time when men began to write more
smoothly and in better rhythm—the Elizabethan
period, when poets like Spenser, courtiers like

Raleigh and Sir Philip Sydney, put their inmost thoughts and feelings into verse.

At the same time, we must remember that hardly any of the hymns written at this time have descended into congregational use at the present day, for they were much more suitable for private than for public worship. It seems strange that, while the Reformation in Germany and other European countries produced a great wave of glorious hymns, in England it seemed rather to banish them. All the beautiful Latin hymns were taken out of the services, in the time of Edward VI., although Archbishop Cranmer had wished to keep them ; and after that hardly any hymns were used in public worship for about three hundred years, except the metrical psalms and the six hymns appended to the Old Version. A national hymn was written by Christopher Barker in 1578, and appended to the Accession Service of Queen Elizabeth's reign, to be sung after evening prayer at all times—

" As for Thy gifts, we render praise."

Then William Hunnis, a gentleman of the Chapel Royal, under Edward VI., and Master of the Children under Elizabeth, wrote hymns. A quaint Elizabethan sacred poem, called *The Highway to Mount Calvarie*, by Samuel Rowlands, begins—

" Up to Mount Calvarie,
If thou desire to goe,
Then take thy crosse and follow Christ,
Thou canst not misse it so."

Spenser's *Hymn of Heavenly Love* would hardly be called a hymn in these days—

> " O Blessed Well of Love ! O Floure of Grace,
> O glorious Morning Starre ! O Lamp of Light !
> Most lively image of Thy Father's Face,
> Eternal King of glorie, Lord of might." etc.

A very beautiful hymn, on the glories of the New Jerusalem, was written during the sixteenth century by an unknown author—a prisoner in the Tower. This hymn, in MS., was signed F. B. P., and some have thought that these initials stood for Francis Baker, Priest—a Roman Catholic who was imprisoned for his faith. The hymn is founded on a passage from S. Augustine, and begins—

> " Jerusalem, my happy home,
> When shall I come to thee?
> When shall my sorrows have an end ?
> Thy joys when shall I see ? "

The hymn is a long one, and many of the verses are very quaint and beautiful, for instance—

> " Quyt through the streets, with silver sound,
> The Flood of Life doth flowe,
> Upon whose banks on every side
> The Wood of Life doth growe.
>
> There trees for evermore bear fruite,
> And evermore doe springe ;
> There evermore the Angels sit,
> And evermore doe singe."

Another hymn, very much like this, was written and published in 1585 by W. Prid, and the title of the book in which it is found is *The Glasse of Vain Glorie*. It is stated that the verses, which number forty-four, are " faithfully translated out of S. Augustine, his book ; " and Prid says, " I have, as near as I could, followed the words of mine author." Some of the stanzas are very much like F. B. P.'s. These are the two last verses—

> "And grant, O Lord, for Christ His sake,
> That once devoide of strife
> I may Thy holy hill attaine
> To dwell in all my life.
>
> With Cherubims, and Seraphims,
> And holy soules of men,
> To sing Thy praise, O Lord of hostes,
> For ever and ever. Amen."

Then a Scotch minister, named David Dickson (1583—1663), wrote another hymn, of two hundred and forty lines, which really combines the two hymns, though some of the stanzas are altered. It begins—

> "O mother dear, Jerusalem,
> When shall I come to thee?"

And about the same time, another version was published in England, altered from that of F. B. P. The last verses show that it was written just after the Restoration (1660)—

> "God still preserve our royal King,
> Our Queen likewise defend,
> And many happy, joyful days,
> Good Lord, unto them send.
>
> Thus to conclude I end my song,
> Wishing health, wealth, and peace,
> And all that wish the Commons' good,
> Good Lord, their ways increase."

There were other versions still, and our hymn—

> "Jerusalem, my happy home,"

remains as a short epitome of them all. There is no doubt that the passage in S. Augustine was the foundation of all. Another favourite hymn, also on the New Jerusalem, written about the same time, and perhaps suggested by the former hymn,

K

was written by a Prebendary of Bristol Cathedral, named Samuel Crossman (1624—1683)—

> " Jerusalem on high,
> My song and city is." (A. & M., 233.)

Our poem is only a part of the original, taken from a poem called *Heaven*.

The earliest attempt at an English hymn-book was George Wither's *Hymns and Songs of the Church*. He obtained a patent from the king, in 1623, that this should be bound up with every copy of the metrical psalms, but this only brought him persecution and loss. The book contains paraphrases of Scripture, hymns for the festivals and for all sorts of occasions ; but with the exception of one or two, these did not survive. The sunset hymn is used still—

> " Behold the sun, that seemed but now
> Enthroned overhead." (A. & M., 476.)

Wither's note to this hymn is—" The singing or meditating to such purposes as are intimated in this hymn when we see the sun declining, does perhaps expel unprofitable musings, and arm against the terrors of approaching darkness." Another volume by Wither contains two hundred and thirty-three hymns for all possible occasions, for instance—" A hymn while we are washing," " A hymn for a house-warming," " For one whose beauty is much praised." Many of the verses are very quaint. One of his hymns, to be sung during Holy Communion, was of two hundred lines, and in defence of it he says that it was "to meet the custom among us, that during the time of administering the Holy Sacrament of the Lord's

Supper, there is some hymn or psalm sung, the
better to keep the thoughts of the communicants
from wandering." The people used to sing this
hymn, sitting, till 1840.

We have heard of Ben Jonson's Carol.[1] He also
wrote a hymn of devotion to God the Father,
beginning—

> "Hear me, O God,
> A broken heart
> Is my best part."

In the next century we have a longer list of
sacred poets, but still no hymn-writers, properly
so called. Dr. Donne, Dean of S. Paul's; Herrick, a poet - priest ; Richard Crashaw, George
Herbert, Jeremy Taylor, Henry Vaughan, Richard
Baxter, and the great poet Milton, all wrote sacred
verses, invaluable for private reading and study, but
not really suitable for singing in church. Dr. Donne,
the famous preacher of his time, certainly wrote,
during a long and painful illness, a hymn to God,
which he caused "to be set to a most grave and
solemn tune, and to be often sung to the organ by
the choristers of S. Paul's Church, in his own
hearing, especially at the evening service"—

> "Wilt Thou forgive that sin where I begin,
> Which was my sin, though it were done before ;
> Wilt thou forgive that sin through which I run,
> And do run still, though still I do deplore.
> When Thou hast done, Thou hast not done,
> For I have more."

Richard Baxter's hymn for the sick-room, written
for his wife, is also a very beautiful one. He was
born November 12, 1615, at Rowton, in Shropshire,

[1] p. 92.

and was the son of a yeoman. He became a clergyman at Kidderminster, and at the age of fifty married a wife of twenty, a very good woman, who was most helpful to him. He was a man of very saintly character, and wrote a book well known by name, *The Saints' Rest*. The hymn, which has comforted many sick people, is—

> " Lord, it belongs not to my care,
>   Whether I die or live." (A. & M., 535.)

He also wrote—

> " Ye holy angels bright." (A. & M., 546.)

Herrick's *Litany to the Holy Spirit* is the only one of his sacred poems which has come down into our hymn-books in a modified form. The original is very quaint, and begins—

> " In the hour of my distress,
>   When temptations me oppress,
>   And when I my sins confess,
>   Sweet Spirit, comfort me."
>   (Ch. Hy., 390.)

George Herbert also wrote hymns and sang them to his viol, but few are suitable for public worship.

> " Let all the world in every corner sing,
>   My God and King" (A. & M., 548),

is one of the best. Nicolas Ferrar, his friend, who lived in retirement at Little Gidding, wrote hymns to be sung at his services, but they are all lost.

Jeremy Taylor, the poet-preacher, as he was called, was born of humble parents, in 1613. He was very clever, and had a most successful career at college ; he was ordained, and afterwards made chaplain to the Earl of Carbery, at Golden Grove, Carmarthenshire, from which his book is named. He was made Bishop of Down and Connor, and died in 1667. There are some festival hymns in the *Golden Grove*—one, a very fine one, being given, with a few alterations, in the Sarum Hymnal—

> " Draw nigh to Thy Jerusalem, O Lord,
>   Thy faithful people cry, with one accord ;
>   Ride on triumphantly ! Behold, we lay
>   Our passions, lusts, and proud wills in Thy way."

Another beautiful hymn, still often used—

> "A living stream, as crystal clear " (A. & M., 213),

was written by the Rev. J. Mason, Rector of Water Stratford, Bucks, who died in 1694.[1]

Now we come to a great man, a hero as well as a hymn-writer—Bishop Ken. He was born at Little Berkhampstead, in Hertfordshire, in 1637, and went to school at Winchester. There, as in after-life, he was noted for his early rising ; and even on the coldest winter mornings would be up long before the other boys. At Oxford, we hear of him as "student, poet, and musician." He wrote a manual for the Winchester scholars, containing some beautiful prayers, and another well-known book, *The Practice of Divine Love*. His famous hymns were written while at Winchester for his own use, and he would sing them in his own musical voice, accompanying himself on the lute— for he played lute, viol, and organ with great

---

[1] This was afterwards adapted by Keble—p. 181.

proficiency. He was made rector of Brightstone, a lovely spot in the Isle of Wight, in 1667. We are told that such was the purity of Ken's mind that those who knew him called him "seraphicus," and "spiritualis." He published four volumes of hymns and poems, but none of these have lived except the well-known Morning, Evening, and Midnight hymns—

> "Awake, my soul, and with the sun"
> (A. & M., 3),
> " Glory to Thee, my God, this night"
> (A. & M., 23),

and that for midnight—

> "My God, now I from sleep awake,
> The sole possession of me take ;
> From midnight terrors me secure,
> And guard my heart from thoughts impure.
>
> Bless'd angels, while we silent lie,
> Your Hallelujahs sing on high,
> Your joyful hymn the ever-blessed,
> Before the throne, and never rest." etc.

In 1683, Ken was made Bishop of Bath and Wells, and then began the terrible time of anxiety for the Church. He spent three days and nights at the death-bed of Charles II., for the king respected him, and used to say he would go and hear Ken "tell him of his faults." Then, in James II.'s reign, followed the Trial of the Seven Bishops, of whom Ken was one, and after which he was deprived of his bishopric. He retired into the country, and his last days are sad to read of. For some time he had suffered from a painful disease, and is said to have carried his shroud about with him in his portmanteau. He died in 1711, at the age of seventy-three, and by his own desire was buried at sunrise, under the east window of the church at Frome. His last declaration deserves to be remembered. " As for my religion, I die in the Holy Catholic and Apostolic Faith, professed by the whole Church before the disunion of East and West ; more particularly I die in the Communion of the Church of England, as it stands distinguished from all Papal and Puritan innovations, and as it adheres to the doctrine of the Cross." These verses are from his epitaph—

" To him is raised no marble tomb,
  Within the dim cathedral fane,
But some faint flowers of summer bloom,
  And silent falls the winter's rain.

No village monumental stone
  Records a verse, a date, a name.
What boots it ? When thy task is done,
  Christian, how vain the sound of fame.

Oh, far more grateful to thy God,
  The voices of poor children rise,
Who hasten o'er the dewy sod
  To pay their morning sacrifice."

XXI.

THE RELIGIOUS REVIVAL OF THE EIGHTEENTH CENTURY.

"It was mostly the hymns," said Toby; "first the Bible, and then mostly the hymns; for they are the Bible, for the most part, only set to music-like, so that it rings in your heart like a tune. Our class-leader is no great speaker; but he's got a wonderful feeling heart, and a fine voice for the hymns; and it's they that has finished Parson Wesley's work, and healed the wound he made."

IT seems strange that nearly all the great hymn-writers of the eighteenth century should have been (with the exception of the Wesleys) Nonconformists. The Church of England had lapsed into a cold, formal state, and many good people left it because they found more life and energy among the Dissenters. The first hymn-writer of the eighteenth century was Isaac Watts, born at Southampton, of Huguenot ancestry, in 1674. He became an Independent minister, and his greatest recreation was verse-making. He wrote altogether between four and five thousand hymns. When a young man of twenty-two, he was sitting at a window at Southampton, looking over the water at the beautiful country beyond, and he thought of another still more beautiful country, and of the water which parts it from us, and he wrote the hymn—

"There is a land of pure delight,
Where saints immortal dwell"
(Ch. Hy., 519; A. & M., 536),

in which come the lines—

> "Death, like a narrow sea, divides
> This heavenly land from ours."

A little story is told about this hymn. During the Crimean War, one bitterly cold night, a poor soldier was suffering such torture from hunger, sickness, and cold, that he had almost made up his mind to put an end to himself, when suddenly he heard a voice singing—

> "There is a land of pure delight."

He called out loudly, and the singer made his way through the blinding snow to the soldier. He was a good man, named Duncan Mathieson, who had lost his way in the storm, and was keeping his spirits up by singing. So he comforted the poor soldier and saved him from his awful thoughts.

Watts is chiefly known as the author of the *Divine Songs*, the only children's hymns our grandparents possessed. They were written for the children of Sir Thomas Abney, with whom he lived for a long time. Many were written in the summer-house of the Hertfordshire garden, and lessons were drawn from the "busy bee," the ant, or the caterpillar, for the children's use. By far the most poetical of these is the Cradle Hymn—

> "Hush, my dear, lie still and slumber,
>   Holy angels guard thy bed ;
> Heavenly blessings without number,
>   Gently falling on thy head.
>
> Soft and easy is thy cradle,
>   Coarse and hard thy Saviour lay,
> When His birthplace was a stable,
>   And His softest bed was hay.

> See the kinder shepherds round Him,
>   Telling wonders from the sky ;
> Where they sought Him, there they found Him,
>   With His Virgin Mother by.
>
> May'st thou live to know and fear Him,
>   Trust and love Him all thy days ;
> Then go dwell for ever near Him,
>   See His Face, and sing His Praise."

But Watts wrote more famous hymns than these—

> "O God, our Help in ages past"
>   (Ch. Hy., 446 ; A. & M., 165),
> "When I survey the wondrous Cross"
>   (Ch. Hy., 547 ; A. & M., 108),

sung through England on New Year's Day and Good Friday, and

> "Come, let us join our cheerful songs
>   With angels round the Throne."
>   (Ch. Hy., 348 ; A. & M., 299.)
> "Jesus shall reign where'er the sun."
>   (Ch. Hy., 407 ; A. & M., 220.)

The last has become a famous missionary hymn. We read of one occasion when it was used, in a country whose king had just exchanged a heathen for a Christian form of worship—

"Under the spreading branches of the banyan-trees sat some five thousand natives, from Tonga, Fiji, and Samoa, on Whitsunday, 1862, assembled for divine worship. Foremost amongst them all sat King George himself. Around him were seated old chiefs and warriors, who had shared with him the dangers and fortunes of many a battle. It would be impossible to describe the deep feeling manifested when the solemn service began by the entire audience singing Dr. Watts' hymn—

'Jesus shall reign where'er the sun.'"

One of Watts' friends, Doddridge—another Independent minister, whose grandfather had escaped from religious persecution in Bohemia, with no other possessions than Luther's Bible and some gold pieces—was also a great hymn-writer. Three of his hymns are still much sung—

"Hark, the glad sound! the Saviour comes"
(Ch. Hy., 68 ; A. & M., 53),

"Ye servants of the Lord" (Ch. Hy., 562 ; A. & M., 208) ;

and, most famous of all, the hymn which was inserted at the end of the Prayer-book at the beginning of the century—

"My God, and is Thy Table spread."
(Ch. Hy., 212 ; A. & M., 317.)

It is a curious fact that, while many in the Church of England still look upon hymns during Holy Communion with suspicion, it was at one time the only occasion when they were used by Nonconformists.

Two well-known hymns were written by John Byrom, born 1691, a Lancashire man, and a good scholar and poet—

"Christians, awake, salute the happy morn"
and   (A. & M., 61),

"My spirit longs for Thee" (Ch. Hy., 436),

the curious part of the hymn being that the last line of each verse forms the first line of the next. Another beautiful Easter hymn of this century, by an unknown author, is—

"Angels, roll the rock away,
·   Death, yield up thy mighty prey.
See ! He rises from the tomb,
Glowing with immortal bloom. Hallelujah.

'Tis the Saviour ; Angels, raise
Fame's eternal trump of praise,
Let the earth's remotest bound
Hear the joy-inspiring sound.   Hallelujah." etc.

But the great leaders of the Evangelical revival
of the eighteenth century were two brothers, John
and Charles Wesley, who, although they never left
the Church themselves, became the founders of the
sect now called Wesleyans.   John Wesley saw at
once that hymns could be utilized, not only to raise
devotion, but to instruct in the faith, and he meant
them to be a kind of creed in verse.   The brothers
were born at Epworth, in Lincolnshire, and their
parents were very good people ; in fact, the mother
of the Wesleys has become famous for her piety,
and for the clever way in which she brought up
her children.   John and Charles were at Oxford
together, and there they formed a little band of
young men uniting together to lead purer, holier
lives, and to attend the Holy Communion, to visit
the poor, to fast and pray.   For this they were
ridiculed by a crowd of undergraduates ; but they
began to influence others, and later on they went
about preaching all over England, and trying to
wake people up from the dead, cold, formal religion
that was so prevalent.   Then it was that the hymns
took so much effect.   They did almost more even
than the preaching, in bending stubborn wills, and
making them feel the love of Christ.   The best
known by Charles Wesley are—

" Hark, the herald angels sing." (A. & M., 60.)
" Hail the day that sees Him rise." (A. & M., 147.)
" Christ, Whose glory fills the skies." (A. & M., 272.)
" O Love Divine, how sweet thou art." (A. & M., 195.)

" Rejoice, the Lord is King." (A. & M., 202.)
" Let saints on earth in concert sing." (A. & M., 221.)
" Love Divine, all love excelling." (A. & M., 520.)
" Shepherd Divine, our wants relieve." (A. & M., 248)
" Soldiers of Christ, arise " (A. & M., 207) ;
and, most famous of all—

" Jesu, Lover of my soul." (A. & M., 193.)

Charles Wesley was a true poet and a perfect
hymn-writer. Looking at any of his hymns, we
shall find that there is no confusion of thought in
them ; one idea is carried through and worked out.
For instance, in the last-named hymn, the idea is
that of a drowning man clinging to his Saviour,
and the analogy is kept up throughout. This
hymn must have been a help to thousands in
danger of body or of mind. There are several
stories of the way in which it has been sung.

" Forty years ago, on a winter's night, a heavy gale set in
upon the precipitous rock-bound coast of one of our western
counties. A brave little coasting-vessel struggled hard and
long to reach some shelter in the Bristol Channel, but the
struggle was vain—one dark, fearful headland could not be
weathered ; the bark must go on shore, and what a shore it
was, the fated men well knew. Then came the last pull for
life. The boat was swung off and manned—captain and
crew united in one more brave effort ; but their toiling at
the oar was soon over—their boat was swamped. They
seem to have sunk together, for in the morning, when the
day dawned, they were found lying all but side by side under
the shelter of a weedy rock. There was no sign of life on
deck, and below scarcely anything told of late distress. One
token of peace there was—the captain's hymn-book still
lying upon the locker, closed upon the pencil with which he
had marked some passages before he left the ship to meet
his fate. A leaf of the page was turned down, and several
pencil-marks were seen on the margin of Charles Wesley's
hymn—

'Jesu, Lover of my soul,
Let me to Thy Bosom fly.'"

"A ship caught fire, and on board, among the passengers, were a father, mother, and child. The father was separated from them in the tumult that followed the breaking out of the flames, and the mother and child fell into the sea. On the afternoon of the same day the crew of another vessel passing by heard a sound of singing, and looking over the water they saw a black speck floating. A boat was lowered, and the sailors who rowed towards the speck heard distinctly over the waves the words—

'Jesu, Lover of my soul,
Let me to Thy Bosom fly.'

They rowed nearer, and at last they saw, clinging to a fragment of the burnt ship, a mother and child. The mother was singing, as she thought, her dying prayer to the Saviour; but her earnest faith and trust saved her and her child, and the two were safely landed in the other ship."

Charles Wesley composed his hymns at all times and seasons—on horseback, in a stage-coach, in a boat; in fact, he says he hardly ever ceased to write them. His Eucharistic hymns are specially fine. Two are given in Hymns A. & M. (554, 556), and another is—

"All hail, Redeemer of mankind,
Thy Life on Calvary resigned,
Did freely once for all atone.
Thy Blood has paid our utmost price,
Thy everlasting sacrifice
Remains eternally alone." etc.

Charles Wesley died in 1788, and was buried in Marylebone Churchyard, for he had said, "I have lived and I die in the Communion of the Church of England, and I will be buried in the yard of my parish church."

A hymn "with a history" we owe to one of the

disciples of the Wesleys, Thomas Olivers. He was born in Montgomeryshire, 1725, and in his early life apprenticed to a shoemaker. He was a wild, reckless youth, and led a bad life until at Bristol he heard Whitfield preach from the text, " Is not this a brand plucked from the burning ?" This sermon changed his whole life, and a little later, at Bradford-on-Avon, he met John Wesley, who made him one of his preachers, and sent him to Cornwall. He worked there until his death in 1799, and was buried in Wesley's tomb, City Road, London. He wrote several hymns, but the one that has made his name famous is—

"The God of Abraham praise."
(Ch. Hy. 511 ; A. & M., 601.)

This is a free rendering of the Hebrew *Yigdal*, or doxology, which tells, in metrical form, the thirteen articles of the Hebrew Creed, and is supposed to have been composed by Daniel ben Judah, a medieval writer. Olivers gave, as far as possible, a Christian character to it. The Yigdal is in the Hebrew prayer-books, and is sung at the end of the Synagogue service on the eve of Sabbaths and festivals, and at family worship in Jewish homes. It may now be heard any Friday evening, chanted to the melody called *Leoni*, after a great public singer of the name—a chorister of the Great Synagogue, Aldgate, London, at the end of last century. Olivers is said to have written the hymn at the house of John Bakewell, at Westminster, 1770 ; and he went to see Leoni, who gave him the Synagogue melody. Montgomery calls this hymn "the noble ode of an unlettered man." He says—

"There is not, in our language, a lyric of more majestic style, more elevated thought, or more glorious imagery.   Its structure, indeed, is unattractive and, on account of its short lines, occasionally uncouth ; but, like a stately pile of architecture severe and simple in design, it strikes less on the first view than after deliberate examination, when its proportions become more graceful, its dimensions expand, and the mind itself grows greater by contemplating it."

Another very well-known hymn, the author of which is unknown, appeared about this time, the favourite Easter hymn—

"Jesus Christ is risen to-day" (A. & M., 134),

probably taken from a Latin hymn of the fourteenth century.

We must not forget Toplady, author of the famous

"Rock of ages, cleft for me." (A. & M., 184.)

He wrote this while dying of consumption, and its title is, "A living and dying prayer for the holiest believer in the world."   It has been translated into Latin by Gladstone, and is sung in many languages almost all over the Christian world.   It comforted the Prince Consort, and no doubt many others in their dying hours.

The "Olney hymns" belong to the eighteenth century.   They were written by the poet Cowper and his friend, John Newton.   The latter had a strange history.   He was born in London in 1725, and as his mother died when he was only seven years old, he was left to grow up anyhow, and fell in with bad companions.   He led a wild life after entering the navy, which he deserted, becoming a slave-trader and captain of a slave-ship.   One day (he was about twenty-four years old) he picked up, during a voyage, a copy of the *Imitation of Christ*, and read it. He thought, "Can these things be true?" And that very night a terrible storm arose, and the ship was nearly wrecked. From that time he led a different life, and when he was thirty-nine he was ordained to the curacy of Olney, where he worked hard for many years. It was there that he met the poet Cowper, and together they composed hymns for a religious meeting held by Newton. A collection of these was published in 1779, and called the Olney Hymns; sixty-eight by Cowper, two hundred and eighty by Newton. Few of these are now left in our modern hymn-books, but three of them have a world-wide fame. One is by Newton—

"How sweet the name of Jesus sounds." (A. & M., 176.)

Cowper was subject to dreadful fits of melancholy, almost amounting to madness. During one of these temporary fits he became possessed with the idea that he should go to a particular part of the river Ouse and drown himself. So he hired a post-chaise and started; but happily the driver missed his way, and as he walked back through the fields the cloud seemed to be lifted from his mind, and he composed a beautiful hymn called, "Light shining out of darkness"—

"God moves in a mysterious way
His wonders to perform."
(Ch. Hy., 257; A. & M., 373.)

But his most touching hymn is—

"Hark, my soul, it is the Lord" (A. & M., 260.)

This gives one a much happier idea of the man;

L

indeed, one who saw him after death said, "With the calmness of the face there mingled, as it were, a holy surprise."

XXII.

BEGINNING OF THE NINETEENTH CENTURY.

"Then Christian gave three leaps for joy and went on singing."—*Pilgrim's Progress.*

ANY one living in Nottingham about the year 1792 might perhaps have seen a little butcher's boy carrying legs of mutton from his father's shop, and following him home as the evening twilight gathered in, and entering the kitchen, might have witnessed rather a remarkable sight. The little fellow, who was only seven years old, sitting with a grave, studious face at the head of the table, while two or three rough-looking servants were poring over the copies he gave them to write, or the letters he was teaching them to form into words. The lad's name was Henry Kirke White. By the time he was seventeen he had published a volume of poems, besides studying law, and learning Latin, Greek, French, Italian, and Spanish. His great ambition was to go to the University, and to be ordained; and after overcoming many difficulties, he entered S. John's College, Cambridge, in the year 1805. But, sad to say, he worked too hard for his strength, and after being first man of his college for two years, it gave way, and he died at the age of twenty-two. After his death the fragment of a hymn was found among his mathematical papers—

"Much in sorrow, oft in woe,
Onward, Christians, onward go ;
Fight the fight, and worn with strife,
Steep with tears the Bread of Life.

Onward, Christians, onward go,
Join the war and face the foe ;
Faint not, much doth yet remain,
Dreary is the long campaign.

Shrink not, Christians, will ye yield ?
Will ye quit the painful field ? "

Thus far the hymn had gone, and it was afterwards completed by a lady, Fanny Maitland, and remains one of our best-known hymns.

One great hymn-writer of the early part of this century was James Montgomery. His parents were Moravians, and after sending their boy to the Moravian school at Fulneck, near Leeds, they went out to the West Indies as missionaries, and died there. They had meant their little son to be a preacher too, but he had made up his mind to be a poet, and although poetry was forbidden at the school, he had written before he was fourteen a poem of one thousand lines. He entered a newspaper office, and afterwards became an editor, and all his life he continued to write poetry. The hymns by Montgomery we know best are—

"Hail to the Lord's Anointed."
(Ch. Hy., 379 ; A. & M., 219.)
"Go to dark Gethsemane." (Ch. Hy., 372 ; A. & M., 110.)

"Lord, teach us how to pray aright."
(Ch. Hy., 370 ; A. & M., 247.)
"Songs of praise the angels sang."
(Ch. Hy., 503 ; A. & M., 297.)
"For ever with the Lord." (Ch. Hy., 363 ; A. & M., 231.)
"Lord, pour Thy Spirit from on high."
(Ch. Hy., 253 ; A. & M., 355.)
"Palms of glory, raiment bright." (A. & M., 445.)

The beautiful penitential hymn—

"In the hour of trial,
Jesus, pray for me" (Ch. Hy., 391),

was written in a lady's album, and dated Dec. 8,
1834. In the MS. the second line is, "Jesus, stand
by me"; but Montgomery altered this afterwards.

Some little stories about his hymns are known.
One day in the month of February 1832, he was
travelling with a friend between Gloucester and
Tewkesbury, when he noticed some women and
girls working in a field lately ploughed. They
were stooping down in rows, but they could not be
weeding. What were they doing? Then he was
told that their work was called *dibbling*, and that,
instead of throwing in the grain broadcast over the
field, holes were pricked in straight lines, and into
each of these holes two or three grains of wheat
were dropped. "Dibbling is unpoetical and un-
picturesque," said Montgomery ; "give me broadcast sowing." And then he began to think about
sowing the good seed—the dibbling of Sunday-
school teaching and visiting—here a little, there
a little ; and the broadcast sowing of the preacher.
Gradually his ideas shaped themselves into verse,
and he wrote the hymn—

"Sow in the morn thy seed,
 At eve hold not thy hand ;
 To doubt and fear give thou no heed,
 Broadcast it o'er the land.

Thou know'st not which may thrive,
 The late or early sown ;
 Grace keeps the chosen germ alive,
 When and wherever strown." etc.

Another hymn, " Eternity, eternity," has a pretty story connected with it. Montgomery was walking one day on the Castle Hill at Scarborough, and stood on the edge of the cliff, meditating. He had with him a little girl, and he had just been telling her the meaning of the word "horizon," and she was wishing she could see it, for a mist hid the meeting of sea and sky. " It is far more sublime as it is," said the poet ; "it is like looking into *eternity.*" "What is eternity?" asked the child. "You have asked a question which none of the wise men in the world can answer," said he ; "God only can comprehend eternity." The child pondered a while, and then said, "I do not like to think about eternity—it stretches my head. I think I shall be so tired of it." "Do not think about it any more, my child," he said, " it stretches all our minds." This was the origin of the hymn.

Two other hymns for Christmas and Easter by Montgomery are—

"Angels from the realms of glory,"
. and
"Come, see the place where Jesus lay." (A. & M., 139.)

Thomas Kelly, the son of an Irish judge, wrote a great many hymns, the best known of which are—

"Through the day Thy love has spared us."
(Ch. Hy., 34; A. & M., 25.)
"The Head that once was crowned with thorns."
(A. & M., 301.)
"We sing the praise of Him Who died."
(Ch. Hy., 542; A. & M., 300.)

Then follow two bishops. The first, Bishop Mant, who died in 1848, was born, like Watts, at Southampton, and became Bishop of Down and Connor, in Ireland. He was a writer both of prose and verse, and to him we owe the fine translation of the *Stabat Mater*—

"At the Cross her station keeping" (A. & M., 117);

also the Good Friday hymn—

"See the destined day arise." (A. & M., 113.)
"Bright the vision that delighted." (A. & M., 161.)

His chief work was translating from the Latin.

There is a good deal more to say about the next bishop—Reginald Heber. His parents were both Yorkshire people, but he was born in Cheshire, in 1783. As a child he was remarkable for the eagerness with which he read the Bible and remembered it after. He was noted in his school-boy days for his gentleness and wonderful kindness of heart. He was so liberal with his pocket-money, that it was found necessary to sew within the linings of his pockets the bank-notes given him for his half-yearly pocket-money, so that he might not give it all away in charity on the road. At Oxford he gained the University prize for his beautiful poem, *Palestine*. After leaving college, Heber went on a tour to Russia and the North before his ordination. He was an excellent parish priest, and felt sorely the need of improving the hymn-singing in churches, for in those days it was very dreary. He composed many hymns at odd moments when not engaged in parish work, and most of them were published after his death. One of the finest of our modern hymns is his—

"Holy, holy, holy, Lord God Almighty."

It is so completely a hymn of adoration. All thought of self is merged in the thought of the holiness and greatness of God. Heber was always very particular to use reverent language in his hymns, for he was shocked at some which contained improper epithets in speaking of God. He generally connected his hymns with the Collect or Gospel for the day in question, and meant them to be sung between the Nicene Creed and the sermon. Some of his finest are—

"Brightest and best of the sons of the morning"
(Ch. Hy., 95);
"Hosanna to the living Lord"
(Ch. Hy., 383; A. & M., 241);
"The Son of God goes forth to war"
(Ch. Hy., 201; A. & M., 439);

and the first verse of the beautiful little evening hymn—

"God, Who madest earth and heaven."
(Ch. Hy., 22; A. & M., 26.)

The second verse was added by Archbishop Whately, some years later, and is founded upon the antiphon—

"Save us, O Lord, while waking, guard us sleeping, that we may watch with Christ, and may repose in peace."

Two beautiful introits by Heber are—

"Oh, most merciful !
Oh, most bountiful !
God the Father Almighty !
By the Redeemer's sweet intercession,
Hear us, help us, when we cry."

"Bread of the world, in mercy broken,
  Wine of the soul, in mercy shed,
By Whom the words of life were spoken,
  And in Whose death our sins are dead ;

Look on the heart by sorrow broken,
  Look on the tears by sinners shed,
And be Thy feast to us the token
  That by Thy grace our souls are fed."
                                    (Ch. Hy., 204.)

Heber wrote a burial hymn, on the death of his
first child, a great grief to him—

"Thou art gone to the grave, but we will not deplore thee,
  Though sorrows and darkness encompass the tomb ;
The Saviour hath passed through its portals before thee,
  And the lamp of His love is thy guide thro' the gloom."

And a fine hymn for sailors—

"When through the torn sail the wild tempest is streaming,
  When o'er the dark wave the red lightning is gleaming,
  Nor hope sends a ray the poor seaman to cherish,
  We fly to our Maker, 'Save, Lord, or we perish !'"

This hymn was written upon the Gospel for the
Fourth Sunday after Epiphany. All through his
life Heber had taken the deepest interest in
missions, and he wrote the missionary hymn—

"From Greenland's icy mountains"
                (Ch. Hy., 290 ; A. & M., 358),

for an S.P.G. service on Whitsunday, 1819.

Four years after this he became Bishop of Cal-
cutta, and went out with his wife to India, to begin
his missionary life. But, sad to say, his splendid

work was very quickly over. On the morning of April 3, 1826, the good bishop had held a Confirmation at a place named Trichinopoly, before breakfast. After it was over, he went to have a cold bath. He did not appear, as usual, directly after it, and his servant went into the room to see what was the matter. To his great distress, he found his master dead in the bath, with his face downwards. A blood-vessel on the brain had burst, and the good bishop was no more.

Heber had intended to publish a collection of hymns connected with the Church's year; but it was not until after his death that this hymn-book was brought out. It contained some very fine hymns by Dean Milman, a son of one of George III.'s physicians. He wrote, for Palm Sunday—

> " Ride on, ride on, in majesty "
> (Ch. Hy., 114; A. & M., 99);

for the Sixteenth Sunday after Trinity—

> " When our heads are bowed with woe "
> (Ch. Hy., 348; A. & M., 399);

for Good Friday, the beautiful Passion hymn—

> " Bound upon the accursed tree,
> Faint and bleeding, Who is He?"

Another hymn-writer of the early part of this century was Sir Robert Grant, born 1785, of an old Scotch family. He was Governor of Bombay, and his two most famous hymns are—

> " O worship the King, all glorious above "
> (Ch. Hy., 477; A. & M., 167);

and the beautiful Litany hymn—

> " Saviour, when in dust to Thee,
> Low we bow the adoring knee."
> (Ch. Hy., 494; A. & M., 251.)

Then came one whose short life was a very holy one—Thomas Whitehead (1815—1843). He went out to New Zealand as chaplain to Dr. Selwyn; but shortly after landing he ruptured a blood-vessel, and never was able to take any duty. He spent what little time and strength remained to him in correcting the Maori translation of the Bible and Prayer-book, and wrote *Seven Hymns towards a Holy Week.* The last, for Saturday, is the best known—

> "Resting from His work to-day,
> In the tomb the Saviour lay." (A. & M., 124.)

Five days before he died he wrote to a friend—

> "I took up the translation of the Evening Hymn into Maori rhyming verse—the first of the kind of the same metre and rhythm as the English. Two hundred and fifty copies have been printed, and sung in church and school by the natives; and several of them came and sang by my window. They call it 'the new hymn of the sick minister.' It is hard to compress Bishop Ken's lines into the same bounds in a rude language. However, it is done, and people seem pleased with it; and it is a comfort to think one has introduced Bishop Ken's beautiful evening hymn into the Maori evening worship, and left them this legacy when I could do no more for them."

The last hymn-poet we shall name is Henry Francis Lyte. He died in consumption, and just after preaching his last sermon wrote a hymn which will probably never die—

> "Abide with me, fast falls the eventide." (A. & M., 27.)

In one of his last poems he wrote—

> "And grant me, swan-like, my last breath to spend
> In songs that may not die."

And the prayer was answered.

XXIII.

AMERICAN HYMNS.

" Brethren of the West, my soul
    Oft to you will westward wing,
When some hymn ascendeth whole,
    At the hour of offering.
Thinking how 'twill onward roll,
    Till your voice the same shall sing ;
Uttered o'er and o'er again,
    Till ye give the last Amen."
                    COXE'S *Christian Ballads.*

IT is a beautiful fact that the song of praise to God never ceases ; for, while we of the English Church are sleeping, our Brethren of the West are singing their early matin or late evening hymns.

" When the gorgeous day begins,
    In the world's remotest East,
And the sun his pathway wins,
    Bringing back some glorious feast,
There, forestalling fears and sins,
    Kneels the faithful English priest,
There the Altar glitters fair,
Spread for Eucharistic prayer.

And, as each meridian line
    Gains the travelled sun that day,
Still begin those rites Divine,
    Still new priests begin to pray ;
Still are blest the Bread and Wine,
    Still one prayer salutes his ray ;
Continent and ocean round
Rolls the tidal wave of sound.

That same hymn, ere I have sung,
    Has been sung in England's fanes,
And perchance, in barbarous tongue,
    'Mid the orient hills and plains,

> And to die, the woods among,
>   Swells from aisles and tinted panes,
>   To the forest's solemn cells,
>   Where the roving red man dwells."

Before the present century hardly any hymns were sung in America—metrical psalms taking their place ; but, during the last fifty or sixty years, not only have our best English hymns found their way there, but many of our own most beautiful hymns come from the "new country." We will speak first of the hymns written by members of the Episcopal Church—our own sister Church. Dr. Mühlenberg (1796—1879), the rector of a church in New York, wrote many hymns, amongst them the beautiful little baptismal hymn—

> " Saviour, Who Thy flock art feeding."
>   (Children's Hy. Bk., 284.)

Mrs. Beecher-Stowe, the popular authoress of *Uncle Tom's Cabin*, composed several hymns, among them the well-known mission hymn (London Mission Hy. Bk., 64)—

> " Knocking, knocking, who is there?
>   Waiting, waiting, oh, how fair ! "

and another—

> " Still, still with Thee, when purple morning breaketh."

Bishop Doane (1799—1859) wrote many hymns, amongst others one for missions— *(sic)*

> " Fling out the banner, let it float,"

and

> " Thou art the Way, to Thee alone
>   From sin and death we flee."
>   (Ch. Hy., 526 ; A. & M., 199.)

And the Rev. Charles William Everest gave us a still better known hymn—

"Take up thy cross, the Saviour said."
(Ch. Hy., 307 ; A. & M., 263.)

Then comes Dr. Coxe, one of whose *Christian Ballads* has been quoted. He is Bishop of the Western Diocese of New York, and wrote the famous missionary hymn—

"Saviour, sprinkle many nations"
(Ch. Hy., 294 ; A. & M., 359),

when on a visit to England. It was begun on Good Friday, 1850, and finished in 1851, in the grounds of Magdalen College, Oxford. He also wrote a hymn for Holy Week, one for S. Bartholomew's Day—

"Behold an Israelite indeed
In whom no guile is found ;"

and one for S. Matthew's Day—

"He who for Christ hath left behind,
Or house, or land, or wife."

In his collection of poems there also occurs a very pretty carol—

"Carol, carol, Christians,
Carol joyfully ;
Carol for the coming
Of Christ's Nativity."

Dr. Coxe also wrote a very good translation of a Latin hymn, supposed to have been written in prison by Mary, Queen of Scots—

"O Blessed Redeemer, I've trusted in Thee,
O Saviour, my Jesu, now liberate me ;
In horrible prison
And gloom have arisen
My sighs, O my Jesu, incessant to Thee ;
But oh ! on my sorrow
Has brightened no morrow,
Yet hear me, my Jesu, and liberate me."

Now we come to the hymns written by those who were not members of the Episcopal Church, and first to the poets, for nearly all the great American poets wrote, at any rate, *one* good hymn.

Whittier, the Quaker poet of anti-slavery (*b.* 1807), began life first as a farm-boy, then as a shoemaker, but he afterwards became a successful journalist and poet. He modestly wrote of himself—" I am really not a hymn-writer, for the good reason that I know nothing of music. A good hymn is the best use to which poetry can be devoted, but I do not claim that I have succeeded in composing one." When we look at some verses from one of his hymns, we shall find, however, that he was not quite just in his estimate of himself—

" We may not climb the heavenly steeps,
    To bring the Lord Christ down,
In vain we search the lowest deeps
    For Him Who fills Heaven's Throne.

But to the contrite spirit yet,
    A present help is He,
And faith has still its Olivet,
    And love its Galilee.

The healing of His seamless dress,
    Is by our beds of pain ;
We touch Him in life's throng and press,
    And we are whole again.

We faintly hear, we dimly see ;
    In differing phrase we pray ;
But, dim or clear, we own in Thee
    The Life, the Truth, the Way."

Oliver Wendell Holmes, the great doctor and novelist (1809—1891), gives us, among his poems, a very fine hymn for Sunday morning—

> " Lord of all being, throned afar,
> Thy glory flames from sun and star ;
> Centre and soul of every sphere,
> Yet to each loving heart how near.

> Our midnight is Thy smile withdrawn,
> Our noontide is Thy gracious dawn :
> Our rainbow arch Thy mercy's sign,
> All, save the clouds of sin, are Thine."

The whole hymn is well worthy of a place in more of our English hymn-books. Dr. Holmes wrote other hymns, one being for soldiers.

We must not forget Longfellow, whose " Hymn for my brother's ordination " is hardly fitted for public use, though very beautiful—

> " Christ to the young man said—' Yet one thing more,
> If thou would'st perfect be ;
> Sell all thou hast, and give it to the poor,
> And come and follow Me.' "

Next on our list come two poetesses—(1) Sarah Elizabeth Miles, who wrote—

> " Thou Who didst stoop below,
> To drain the cup of woe,
> And wear the form of frail mortality ;
> Thy blessed labours done,
> Thy crown of victory won,
> Hast passed from earth, passed to Thy home on high.

> It was no path of flowers,
> Through this dark world of ours,
> Beloved of the Father, Thou didst tread ;
> And shall we, in dismay,
> Shrink from the narrow way,
> When clouds and darkness are around it spread?" etc.

(2) Adelaide Proctor was a Roman Catholic, but amongst her *Legends and Lyrics* there is a very beautiful evening hymn—

"The shadows of the evening hours
Fall from the darkening sky ;
Upon the fragrance of the flowers
The dews of evening lie ;
Before Thy Throne, O Lord of Heaven,
We kneel at close of day ;
Look on Thy children from on high,
And hear us while we pray.
Let peace, O Lord, Thy peace, O God,
Upon our souls descend,
From midnight fears and perils, Thou
Our trembling hearts defend ;
Give us a respite from our toil,
Calm and subdue our woes ;
Through the long day we suffer, Lord,
O give us now repose."

Others of her poems are used as hymns.

Bryant and Emerson also wrote hymns, but they are not well known in England.

Edmund Sears gave us two well-known Christmas hymns—

"Calm on the listening ear of night,"

and

"It came upon the midnight clear."

A great many of our most popular mission hymns come from America. Horatio Palmer, a doctor of music, wrote the hymn—

"Yield not to temptation,
For yielding is sin ; "

but his namesake, Dr. Ray Palmer (*b*. 1808), the son of a judge in Rhode Island, is the author of a much more famous hymn, as well known in America as "Rock of Ages" in England. It was written in 1830, and he says—"I gave form to what I felt, by writing, with little effort, these stanzas. I recollect I wrote them with very tender emotion, and ended the last line with tears." It begins—

> " My faith looks up to Thee,
> Thou Lamb of Calvary,
>   Saviour Divine.
> Now hear me when I pray,
> Take all my guilt away,
> O let me from this day
>   Be wholly Thine.
>
> While life's dark maze I tread,
> And griefs around me spread,
>   Be Thou my guide ;
> Bid darkness turn to day,
> Wipe sorrow's tears away,
> Nor let me ever stray
>   From Thee aside.
>
> When ends life's transient dream,
> When death's cold sullen stream
>   Shall o'er me roll ;
> Blest Saviour, then in love,
> Fear and distrust remove,
> O bear me safe above,
>   A ransomed soul." (Hymn. Comp., 202.)

On the eve of one of the most fearful battles of the American civil war, some six or eight young soldiers had assembled in a tent for prayer. They knew quite well they might die in the battle, and they wished their friends to know that they had died in the faith of Christ, so one of them wrote out this hymn, and each man signed his name at the bottom of the paper. Only one survived the battle, and he told the story. Dr. Palmer wrote several other poems and hymns, notably a beautiful translation of part of S. Bernard's hymn—

> " Jesu, Thou joy of loving hearts."
>   (Ch. Hy., 402 ; A. & M., 177.)

M

Another famous mission hymn—

"Return, O wanderer, to thy home" (A. & M., 628),

was written by Thomas Hastings, a doctor of music, who did a great deal for church music and choirs. Then Philip Bliss, a Congregationalist, who died in a railway accident in 1876 while trying to save his wife, is well known by his favourite hymns—

"Ho, my comrades, see the signal,"
"Light in the darkness, sailor,"
"Only an armour-bearer,"

and many others in mission hymn-books.

We also know the origin of the hymn—

"Shall we gather at the river?"

Robert Lowry, a Baptist minister, was sitting in his room in Brooklyn, New York, one day at a time when an epidemic was raging, and many people in mourning were passing along the street, and the question began to rise in his heart—"Shall we meet again? We are parting at the river of death, shall we meet at the river of life?" So he seated himself at his organ, and the words and music seemed to flow out, as he tells us, by inspiration.

There is quite a long list of American lady hymn-writers, beginning with Anna Warner, the authoress of *The Wide, Wide World*, and *Carl's Christmas Stocking*. In the latter story there is a very pretty child's hymn—

"O little child, lie still and sleep,
  Jesus is near, thou need'st not fear,

No one need fear whom God doth keep
By day or night ;
Then lay thee down, in slumber deep,
Till morning light."

Miss Warner also translated many hymns, and edited a little book, *Hymns of the Church Militant.* Next we have a *blind* hymn-writer, Francis Jane Crosby (Mrs. Van Alstyne). When six weeks old she lost her sight, and was brought up at the New York Blind Institute. She became a teacher there, and afterwards married Alexander Van Alstyne, a musician, and also blind. She wrote a great many poems, and more than two thousand songs and hymns, many of which have become very popular.

"Safe in the arms of Jesus"

was written in 1868, at the request of Mr. W. H. Doane, to his popular melody, and he also wrote tunes to twenty of her hymns. Others, well known, are—

"Rescue the perishing, care for the dying."
"All the way my Saviour leads me."
"A blessing for you, will ye take it ?"
"Revive Thy work, O Lord."
"Pass me not, O gentle Saviour."

Mary Baker wrote the popular mission hymn—

"Master, the tempest is raging,"

which has been sung at many festival services, among others, at that of Garfield. We will conclude with the beautiful little evening hymn, by John Leland, a Baptist minister, well known by the last verse—

" The day is past and gone,
The evening shades appear,
O may we all remember well
The night of death draws near.

We lay our garments by,
Upon our beds and rest,
So death shall soon disrobe us all
Of what is here possest.

Lord, keep us safe this night,
Secure from all our fears,
May angels guard us while we sleep,
Till morning light appears."

XXIV.

MODERN ENGLISH HYMNS.

" Such as found out musical tunes, and recited verses in
writing."—ECCL. xliv. 5.

PERHAPS we hardly realize, even now, how much
hymns helped on the Church revival of the present
century. We can only mention a few of the leading
names of those who wrote them, and we may begin
with a group of three—Keble, Williams, and Neale.

Keble was one of the hymn-poets who lived in
a quiet country place, and wrote amid the scent of
the flowers and the songs of the birds. He was
Vicar of Hursley, in Hampshire, where, in the year
1866, he was buried. His descriptions of scenery
and of nature are most beautiful, and his mind was
so imbued with the Bible, that he describes the
Holy Land almost as if he had seen it. He was

more of a poet than a hymn-writer; but, although we do not use *many* of his hymns in public worship, we could ill spare those which have become almost household words. Those for morning and evening—

"New every morning is the love"
  (Ch. Hy., 8 ; A. & M., 4),
"Sun of my soul, Thou Saviour dear"
  (Ch. Hy., 29 ; A. & M., 24),
"Blest are the pure in heart"
  (Ch. Hy., 339 ; A. & M., 261),
"The voice that breathed o'er Eden"
  (Ch. Hy., 241 ; A. & M., 350),
"A living stream, as crystal clear"[1]
  (A. & M., 213) ;

and, besides several others, the beautiful translation of the lamp-lighting hymn of the early Church—

"Hail, gladdening Light." (A. & M., 18.)

One of Keble's friends and fellow-curates was the Rev. Isaac Williams (1802—1865). At Oxford he obtained the prize for Latin verse, and this threw him at once into close companionship with Keble, who looked over the poem for him ; and afterwards he spent all his long vacations with his "spiritual father," as he called him. Williams stands very high as a devotional writer, both in prose and verse ; he translated many Greek and Latin hymns, and composed original ones. Translations—

"Disposer Supreme." (Ch. Hy., 356 ; A. & M., 431.)
"O heavenly Jerusalem." (A. & M., 429.)
"Morn of morns, and day of days." (A. & M., 33.)
"O Word of God above." (A. & M., 395.)

---

[1] An adaptation of Mason's hymn, p. 149.

Originals—
> "Lord, in this Thy mercy's day."
>> (Ch. Hy., 419; A. & M., 94.)
>
> "Be Thou my Guardian and my Guide."
>> (A. & M., 282.)

Then we come to a man to whom English hymnody owes more, perhaps, than any one else in this century—John Mason Neale (1818—1866). He founded the well-known sisterhood at East Grinstead, and spent most of his life in retirement there. His translations of the early Latin and Greek hymns are wonderful, for he always managed to keep close to the original, and yet to put so much fire and spirit into the English renderings, that they hardly seem like translations. A little illustration shows what power he had in this way. One day, Keble, with whom he was staying, had to go out of the room to fetch something, and when he came back, Neale said, "Why, Keble, I thought you always told me that the *Christian Year* was original." "Yes," he said, "it certainly is." "Then how comes this?" and Neale placed before him the Latin of one of Keble's poems. Keble could not understand it, until at last Neale relieved him by telling him it was his own. Neale's hymns and translations are too numerous to mention.

Christopher Wordsworth, Bishop of Lincoln, nephew of the poet Wordsworth, was one of our greatest modern hymn-writers. He was born in 1807, and died 1885 ; but most of his hymns were published about twenty years before, in a little volume called the *Holy Year*, containing hymns for all the Sundays and Church seasons. Words-

worth was not perhaps such a poet as Keble, but he
was a better hymn-writer: some of his hymns are
very grand and inspiring, and more like the old
Latin hymns than many of our modern ones. Like
the Wesleys, the good bishop looked upon hymns
as a valuable means of making people remember
the doctrines of the Church, and thought the first
duty of a hymn-writer to teach sound doctrine.
Like the Greek hymn-writers, he loved to interpret
the Bible mystically, and thought that materials
for hymns should be found in the Bible, and in old
Christian writings and poetry. Some of his best-
known hymns are—

> " Songs of thankfulness and praise."
>> (Ch. Hy., 100 ; A. & M., 81.)
> "O day of rest and gladness."
>> (Ch. Hy., 45 ; A. & M., 36.)
> "Alleluia, Alleluia ! hearts to heaven and voices raise."
>> (Ch. Hy., 127 ; A. & M., 137.)
> " See the Conqueror mounts in triumph."
>> (Ch. Hy., 147 ; A. & M., 148.)
> "Gracious Spirit, Holy Ghost."
>> (Ch. Hy., 274 ; A. & M., 210.)

A beautiful Trinity Sunday hymn, not so well
known, is—

> " Holy, Holy, Holy, Lord,
> God of hosts, eternal King,
> By the heavens and earth adored,
> Angels and archangels sing ;
> Chanting everlastingly
> To the blessed Trinity."

A little group of English priests, who, within a
year or two of each other (between 1845 and 1847),
joined the Church of Rome, were all fine hymn-

writers—Faber, Newman, and Caswall. Faber was
a poet first, a theologian after. When he told
Wordsworth that he was going to be ordained into
the Anglican Church, Wordsworth remarked—"I
do not say that you are wrong, but England loses
a poet." After he had joined the Church of Rome,
and had found out the power of song, and how
hymn-singing had stirred Christians in all times,
he started the practice of singing in the oratory.
Some favourite hymns by Faber are—

"Sweet Saviour, bless us ere we go."
"O Paradise, O Paradise."
"Hark, hark, my soul."
"O come and mourn with me awhile."
"Jesu, gentlest Saviour."

Cardinal Newman wrote most of his verses while
travelling abroad, in Italy. His most famous
hymns are—

"Lead, kindly light."
"Praise to the Holiest in the height."

Edward Caswall wrote the fine hymn—

"Days and moments quickly flying".;

but his chief *forte* lay in translation, some of the
best being—

"When morning gilds the skies."
"The sun is sinking fast."
"Jesu, the very thought of Thee."
"Glory be to Jesus."

We must not enter on the lists of *living* hymn-
writers, but we may mention one or two of the
women who have immortalized themselves by their
hymns.

Harriet Auber (1773 — 1862) gave us a rich heritage in

"Our blest Redeemer ere He breathed." (A. & M., 207.)

Charlotte Elliot, an invalid lady, left us—

"My God, my Father, while I stray." (A. & M., 264.)
"Just as I am, without one plea." (A. & M., 255.)
"Christian, seek not yet repose." (A. & M., 269.)

Miss Havergal—

"Thy Life was given for me." (A. & M., 259.)
"Thou art coming, O my Saviour." (A. & M., 203.)
"Lord, speak to me, that I may speak" (A. & M., 356) ;

and many others. She wrote all her hymns prayerfully, and she says—

"Writing is praying with me. I never seem to write even a verse by myself, and feel like a little child writing. You know how a little child would look up at every sentence and say, 'And what shall I say next?' That is just what I do. I ask that at every line He would give me, not merely thought and power, but also every word—even the very rhyme."

Mrs. Alderson, a sister of the late Dr. Dykes, left us the beautiful Passion and Almsgiving hymns—

"And now, beloved Lord, Thy soul resigning."
                                        (A. & M.; 121.)
"Lord of glory, Who hast bought us."
                                        (A. & M., 367.)

This short account of hymns and their stories cannot end better than by showing how, in modern times, we have proof of the immense value of hymns in foreign missions in all parts of the world. It is quite wonderful to find how they have helped the work of missionaries. To begin with the North Pole! The Greenlanders have had their own printed hymn-book since 1772, introduced by the Moravian missionaries, and they often sing in their boats, as well as in their churches. Then, in Labrador, a Greenlander, named Jans Haven, in the year 1770, sang to the Eskimos a hymn in his own language, which they understood, and "in the midst of a barbaric dance they were charmed by it into silence." They now sing Christian hymns at morning and evening prayer, and have a book of about nine hundred, translated for them.

Hymns have been found of great use in British Columbia, Queen Charlotte's Islands, Vancouver Island, the Sandwich Islands, Polynesia, the Caroline Islands, the Solomon Islands, Loyalty Islands, Borneo and Singapore, and have been translated into the native languages. The Fiji Islanders possess a book of one hundred and seventy-eight hymns, and delight in singing them. In Bishop Patteson's district, the Norfolk Islands, etc., there is a book of sixty-seven hymns, twenty-five of which are by the martyr-bishop himself. In Japan the work of translating and adapting has been very difficult, because the Japanese poetry has no rhyme nor metre like ours; but, in spite of this, there are at least five Japanese hymn-books, and three hundred and fifty hymns.

It was also found difficult to introduce congregational singing, as, in the Buddhist services, the priests alone chant. The first Chinese hymn-book was published in 1818, and contained thirty hymns, and now there are many more. In India, also, hymns have been much used. In some places the school-children learn to sing them, and so introduce

them to their families; and in others, the missionaries have introduced Christian Kirttans. These
are, really, musical performances, in honour of some
god, by the Hindoos; and some of the native
teachers have written choruses, to be sung in the
same way by Christian singers, and so attracted
the people.

Then, coming to Africa, we find hymns in the
native dialect of Madagascar, Mauritius, Basuto-
land, Zululand, Natal, Cape Colony, Kaffirland,
etc. One of the earliest Christian Kaffir converts
composed a most remarkable hymn, in pure Kaffir
rhythm, beginning, "Thou art the great God, He
Who is in heaven"; which, together with the traditional music, is unique. We cannot do better
than finish with a hymn story from the life of one
of our noblest missionaries—James Hannington,
Bishop of Eastern Equatorial Africa.

This great and good man had gone off upon a
missionary journey, and had come to the territory
of a chieftain who was in deadly enmity to the
Christians. He knew that his life was in danger,
but he was perfectly calm about it—where he felt
it his duty to go, he went; and nothing and nobody
could make him swerve from what he considered
to be the path of duty. Hannington was fond of
singing, and those who were with him in that
perilous journey tell us that "ever and anon his
emphatic voice would be raised in the notes of
some old familiar tune, and the wilderness would
ring to the sound of a Christian hymn."

One of his favourites was—

"Peace, perfect peace, in this dark world of sin."

(A. & M., 537.)

At last he was taken prisoner by the wicked king, and he knew that his end was near. He says—

"Suddenly about twenty ruffians fell on us, and threw me to the ground. Feeling that I was being dragged away, to be murdered at a distance, I sang, ' Safe in the arms of Jesus,' and then laughed at the very agony of the situation."

He died a martyr's death. At the same time three native Christian lads were taken prisoners.

"They were tortured; their arms were cut off, and they were bound alive to the scaffolding, under which a fire was made, and so they were *slowly burned to death*. As they hung in their protracted agony over the flames, Myasi (the wicked king) and his men stood around jeering, and told them to pray *now* to Jesus Christ, if they thought that He could do anything to help them. The spirit of the martyrs at once entered into these lads, and together they raised their voices and praised Jesus in the fire, singing till their shrivelled tongues refused to form the sound, *Killa siku tunsifu*—a hymn translated into the musical language of Uganda. These were the words they sang—

> ' Daily, daily, sing to Jesus,
>   Sing, my soul, His praises due ;
> All He does deserves our praises,
>   And our deep devotion too :
> For in deep humiliation,
>   He for us did live below ;
> Died on Calvary's Cross of torture,   •
>   Rose to save our souls from woe.' "

INDEX OF AUTHORS.

INDEX OF HYMNS.

THE END.

Richard Clay & Sons, Limited, London & Bungay.

PUBLICATIONS

OF THE

Society for Promoting Christian Knowledge.

BOOKS BY

MRS. RUNDLE CHARLES.

"By Thy Cross and Passion."
Thoughts on the words spoken around and on the Cross. Post 8vo. *Cloth boards*, 1*s*. 6*d*.

"By Thy Glorious Resurrection and Ascension."
Easter Thoughts. Post 8vo. *Cloth boards*, 1*s*. 6*d*.

"By the Coming of the Holy Ghost."
Thoughts for Whitsuntide. Post 8vo. *Cloth boards*, 1*s*. 6*d*.

The True Vine.
Post 8vo. *Cloth boards*, 1*s*. 6*d*.

The Great Prayer of Christendom.
Post 8vo. *Cloth boards*, 1*s*. 6*d*.

An Old Story of Bethlehem.
One link in the great Pedigree. Fcap. 4to, with six plates, beautifully printed in colours. *Cloth boards*, 2*s*. 6*d*.

Three Martyrs of the Nineteenth Century.
Studies from the Lives of Livingstone, Gordon, and Patteson. Crown 8vo. *Cloth boards*, 3*s*. 6*d*.

Martyrs and Saints of the First Twelve Centuries.
Studies from the Lives of the Black-letter Saints of the English Calendar. Crown 8vo. *Cloth boards*, 5*s*.

Against the Stream.
The Story of an Heroic Age in England. With eight page woodcuts. Crown 8vo. *Cloth boards*, 4*s*.

Conquering and to Conquer.
A Story of Rome in the days of St. Jerome. With four page woodcuts. Crown 8vo. *Cloth boards*, 2*s*. 6*d*.

Lapsed not Lost.
A Story of Roman Carthage. Crown 8vo. *Cloth boards*, 2*s*. 6*d*.

Sketches of the Women of Christendom.
Crown 8vo. *Cloth boards*, 3*s*. 6*d*.

Miscellaneous Publications.

A Dictionary of the Church of England.
By the Rev. E. L. CUTTS, Author of "Turning-Points of Church
History," &c. With numerous Woodcuts. Crown 8vo.
7s. 6d.

Aids to Prayer.
By the Rev. DANIEL MOORE. Printed in red and black.
Post 8vo. 1s. 6d.

Being of God (Six Addresses on the).
By C. J. ELLICOTT, D.D., Bishop of Gloucester and Bristol.
Small Post 8vo. 1s. 6d.

Bible Places; or, The Topography of the Holy Land.
By the Rev. CANON TRISTRAM. With Map and numerous
Woodcuts. Crown 8vo. 4s.

Called to be Saints.
The Minor Festivals Devotionally Studied. By CHRISTINA
G. ROSSETTI, Author of "Seek and Find." Post 8vo. 5s.

Case for "Establishment" stated (The).
By the Rev. T. MOORE, M.A. Post 8vo. *Paper boards.* 6d.

Christians under the Crescent in Asia.
By the Rev. E. L. CUTTS, B.A., Author of "Turning-Points of
Church History," &c. With numerous Illustrations.
Crown 8vo. 5s.

Daily Readings for a Year.
By ELIZABETH SPOONER. Crown 8vo. 3s. 6d.

Devotional (A) Life of Our Lord.
By the Rev. EDWARD L. CUTTS, B.A., Author of "Pastoral
Counsels," &c. Post 8vo. 5s.

Golden Year, The.
Thoughts for every month. Original and Selected. By EMILY
C. ORR, Author of "Thoughts for Working Days." Printed
in red and black. Post 8vo. 1s. 6d.

Gospels (The Four).
Arranged in the Form of an English Harmony, from the Text
of the Authorized Version. By the late Rev. J. M. FULLER.
With Analytical Table of Contents and Four Maps. 1s.

Holy Eucharist, The Evidential Value of the.

Being the Boyle Lectures for 1879 and 1880. By the Rev.
G. F. MACLEAR, D.D. Third Edition, Revised and
Corrected. Crown 8vo. *Cloth boards,* 4s.

Land of Israel (The).

A Journal of Travel in Palestine, undertaken with special
reference to its Physical Character. By the Rev. Canon
TRISTRAM. With Two Maps and numerous Illustrations.
Large Post 8vo. *Cloth boards,* 10s. 6d.

Lectures on the Historical and Dogmatical Position of the Church of England.

By the Rev. W. BAKER, D.D. Post 8vo. *Cloth boards,* 1s. 6d.

Paley's Evidences.

A New Edition, with Notes, Appendix, and Preface. By the
Rev. E. A. LITTON. Post 8vo. *Cloth boards,* 4s.

Paley's Horæ Paulinæ.

A New Edition, with Notes, Appendix, and Preface. By the
Rev. J. S. HOWSON, D.D., Dean of Chester. Post 8vo.
Cloth boards, 3s.

Peace with God.

A Manual for the Sick. By the Rev. E. BURBIDGE, M.A.
Post 8vo. *Cloth boards,* 1s. 6d.

"Perfecting Holiness."

By the Rev. E. L. CUTTS, B.A. Post 8vo. *Cloth boards,* 2s. 6d.

Plain Words for Christ.

Being a Series of Readings for Working Men. By the late
Rev. R. G. DUTTON. Post 8vo. *Cloth boards,* 1s.

Readings on the First Lessons for Sundays and Chief Holy Days.

According to the New Table. By the Rev. PETER YOUNG.
Crown 8vo. *In two volumes,* 6s.

Religion for Every Day.

Lectures for Men. By the Right Rev. A. BARRY, D.D. Fcap.
8vo. *Cloth boards*, 1s.

Salutary Doctrine.

By C. J. ELLICOTT, D.D., Bishop of Gloucester and Bristol.
Small Post 8vo. *Cloth boards*, 1s. 6d.

Seek and Find.

A Double Series of Short Studies of the Benedicite. By
CHRISTINA G. ROSSETTI. Post 8vo. *Cloth boards*, 2s. 6d.

Servants of Scripture (The).

By the late Rev. JOHN W. BURGON, B.D. Post 8vo. *Cloth
boards*, 1s. 6d.

Some Chief Truths of Religion.

By the Rev. EDWARD L. CUTTS, B.A., Author of "St.
Cedd's Cross," &c. Crown 8vo. *Cloth boards*, 2s. 6d.

Verses.

By CHRISTINA G. ROSSETTI. Post 8vo. Printed in red and
black on hand-made paper. *Cloth boards* 3s. 6d.

LONDON:

NORTHUMBERLAND AVENUE, CHARING CROSS, W.C. ;

43, QUEEN VICTORIA STREET, E.C.

www.ingramcontent.com/pod-product-compliance
Lightning Source LLC
Chambersburg PA
CBHW020625030726

47497CB00007B/2421